Bore Tide

By Wayne L. Vance

Produced by Grey's Creek Publishers
in association with ECPrinting

Printed in the U.S.A. by ECPrinting.com
Eau Claire, WI
1-888-832-1135

ISBN: 978-0-9821688-0-6

About the Author

Wayne Vance has been in Alaska since 1975, when he was assigned to the Air Force forward air control squadron at Fort Richardson. In 1983, he switched professions to join the Anchorage Police Department and retired in 2003, as a police lieutenant in command of the swing shift division.

Mr. Vance now lives with his wife, Carol at Rustic Wilderness Air Park in Willow where they built their retirement home. There he spends time enjoying the Alaskan experience. Between his writing and travels, he also constructs and flies experimental aircraft.

This is his first journey into the field of writing novels and he is continuing work on two other titles to be published in the near future under his publishing company, Grey's Creek Publishers. He can be reached at their e-mail: Northstar@mtaonline.net or HC89 Box 290 Willow, AK 99688

Acknowledgement

I would like to gratefully acknowledge the editing efforts and uncompromising belief in my abilities as a writer by my wife, Carol, and friends Charlene Stewart, and Shirley Winther, who helped make this work possible.

TABLE OF CONTENTS

CHAPTER I
FINDING PORT

It was a golden era when dying sounds of tall ships echoed upon the wind. A new paradigm of modern technology drowns out ghostly cries of the old and new realities were being born in a time of civil war. Captain Alexander Grafton was a man who could still hear the old song even as the world transformed around him. In every great age and every forgotten era, some individuals remain dedicated to tradition and destiny until they too fade into history. Time ushered in steam power, and the industrial revolution changed everything; everything that is except mighty men with tall ships who still had a dream.

****

The two mast sailing brig, Bore Tide, turned to port and began to enter New York's harbor late in the afternoon on a hot July day in the year of our Lord 1863. A stiff breeze filled the partially reefed sails and the beautiful craft crept along with the rolling waves.

The ship had been commissioned by James Grafton and built in 1856, with a design suited for trade in the shallow waters among the islands of the West Indies. She had a raised aft deck by the helm with a stairway which ran down to the Captain's quarters and private mess. Glass surrounded the stern, providing a glorious view aft from his quarters and office. A wide stair ran forward to the center deck where the first and second officer had cabins in front of the Master's quarters and officers' galley

The center deck supported the main mast, cargo hold area and left room for life boats with two launches. Above deck in the bow was the first of two bunk areas and a galley mess for a crew of 17 men. In front, below the main deck was a room for another 25 men. Hiding behind closed portal doors, six defensive cannons lined each side of the hull.

She had two large square mast sails amidships with top sails, and six schooner, or gaff sails forward. One large schooner boom sail aft with four oversized jib sails on the bow made her easily capable of 12 knots in a good wind and highly maneuverable in any sea. Fully rigged she could carry 5400 square feet of sail and run with most steamers of her day.

In any century or in any age, and by all accounts, she was a beautiful ship that reflected the love of her captain and care of her crew. The Bore Tide's captain now stood on the aft deck with his first officer, Mr. Cole, and watched the approach of the harbor. Mr. Dobbs, second officer, leaned over the rail and scoped the line of ships to search for the Breakwater at berth.

At thirty-two years old, Captain Grafton was a tall man and had a solid build. With dashing looks and a clean shave, he was out of style and odd for his day. He had brown hair and jet black eyes that could look straight through a man and seemingly into the soul itself. His hair was also out of style but boded well for his position and nature. Pulled back into a short pony tail, tied in a red ribbon it looked as if he fit better into 17th century colonial America.

His standard dress was a pair of form fitting black wool pants, and black leather flat soled boots with side buttons raising to the mid calf over top his trousers. His look was usually accented by a light colored shirt covered with an open leather waist jacket, slightly longer in the back and folded up, held by two buttons. It had a high stiff collar to fend off the wind and brass buttons down the front rarely snapped. He had had it fashioned in England after a 16th century British Officer's coat which he'd admired.

His waist belt sported a short naval officer's sword on the left. It had an African ivory handle with a gold arbor which was secured in a black sheath. On the right was a short 36 Navy Colt, butt forward with ivory grips in an open holster. The entire belt was covered by a four inch wide red sash which trailed down the length of his saber.

Sticking out from the center of the sash was the handle of a double-edged dagger with a black onyx handle studded in exotic jewels. Unseen, a derringer was hidden along side. Whenever the weather was inclement he covered his outfit with a mid thigh black leather coat lined with a red wool cloth and he wore a British mid-shipman's naval officer's cap.

Mr. Dobbs stood up straight and spun on one heel to shout back over his shoulder. "There she is Mr. Cole, fifth one in on pier six and it looks like we can get in along side."

"Douse sails Mr. Dobbs," Cole replied. "And set out the long boats with line."

"Aye Sir!" Dobbs answered and snapped shut his spy glass before he headed downstairs to the main deck.

Mr. Cole turned around and saw the Captain watching his men work in the mast's rigging. "Looks like this will be a good trip and a solid profit." He remarked.

Slowly he moved his gaze from overhead to Cole's eyes to answer. 'Indeed Mr. Cole," he paused. "Bring us along side the Breakwater and signal her captain." Grafton turned and walked down the steps to his cabin without further comment.

Bass Cole returned to his duties and started to direct the men. He and the Captain had been together since their early days aboard Grafton's father's ship, the Rip Tide. It sailed the Pacific Ocean and traded between the Orient and the West Coast of America. Grafton had always been his hero and mentor. At only 26, Cole had become an accomplished seaman and solid first officer.

He was a slight built man of 5'7" about normal for the time. Cole was also a clean shaven man with blond thinning hair styled after his captain's. On watch today he was dressed as always, in dark wool clothing and a starched white shirt decorated with a black ribbon tie. It was all neatly packed under a long blue overcoat with brass buttons. His double-breasted coat clung snug to his slim waist by a belt which held a sword and Navy Colt. His crisp and clean outfit was topped off with a naval style officer cap.

The men of the Bore Tide's crew were anxious to off load and exchange their cargo with the Breakwater. It meant a voyage end with pay and high times in port before shipping back out. For Grafton's company it meant another huge war profit. The elder Grafton had always been opposed to profiteering in neutral waters and war zones but not so for his son.

With the death of his father in 1859 and the coming of the American Civil War, Grafton saw an opportunity to expand his markets into America's southern harbors by using the Bore Tide to run the Union Blockade against the Confederacy. She was uniquely suited to the task being fast, maneuverable and of shallow draft, useful in the James and Mississippi River outlets.

Employing his other two ships, the Rip Tide and the Breakwater, he'd shuttled contraband cargo between England, Holland and

America. In New York those supplies were transferred to the Bore Tide then smuggled into ports at Richmond and New Orleans. Exchange of goods made profit possible as the Confederate money had quickly become near worthless.

On this trip the Bore Tide was laden with cotton, tobacco, molasses and whiskey all bound for Europe. She would exchange it with barrels of gunpowder (marked flour), cannon barrels (marked machine parts) and wheels with caissons (marked farm implements) from the Breakwater and sail back to Richmond.

For his day, Grafton had become a wealthy man and his war time business boomed. That was, of course, as long as he did not get caught by the U.S. Navy in the exchange of cargo with Confederates. They looked on his lucrative transactions with the same disdain as that of pirates who attacked on the high seas. However, being a Dutch national and immune from war crimes, the major risk was to be boarded at sea and to lose his ship.

Shortly before sunset the men had the Bore Tide berthed along side the Breakwater and the crew was busily securing lines. Three men lowered a gang plank between the two craft amid ships while Captain Grafton waited to cross. "There you be Captain, all secure," one of the men smiled at his boss.

"Thank you, Mr. Quintin," he replied and stepped up onto the wide board to cross over. "Permission to come aboard?" He asked the crewman on the Breakwater, but did not wait for an answer to step onto the deck.

"Welcome aboard, Captain Grafton. Captain Beckett is in his aft cabin and expects you for supper," the man replied before he motioned with his arm to his captain's quarters.

Grafton went to the Captain's door and knocked, "Come in and welcome." A gruff deep voice echoed from behind the door. "Aw yes, Captain Grafton, so good to see you again. I hope everything is well with you?" Captain Beckett smiled and raised his massive frame out of the chair behind his mess table to offer his hand in friendship.

Grafton took the older man's hand, suspecting he had put on some weight since their last meeting. He had been a friend to his father and was the master's mate on the Rip Tide while Grafton grew up at sea. His old English uniform had an unkempt look about it and his long hair and full grey beard covered a very bad complexion.

Grafton had never been taken much by this gruff elderly man, but he was an able sea captain and had earned the right to command the Breakwater by his long service. It had never set well with Beckett when James Grafton put his young son in command over him on the Rip Tide just prior to his own death. Although, upon that death, the younger Grafton did promote him to captain of the Breakwater, yet tensions still lingered between the two men.

"I try to keep the wind to my back," Grafton smiled. "And you Sir, I trust you have been well."

"Yes, yes," he laughed and patted himself on the stomach. "Can't you tell my boy?" He motioned for him to sit at his table while he picked up a bottle of Port to fill a glass. Beckett sat back down with a thud. He took a long pull on his glass of Port which left behind a wet stain on his beard, then banged the goblet back on the table. "We unloaded most of our cargo over the past two days," he explained with a belch, "but the clandestine crates and boxes are still in the hold," he belched again and leaned forward on the wooden table to pass wind.

Ignoring the information for the moment, he smiled at the old man's lack of table manners. Grafton changed the subject, "have you heard from George since you've been in port?"

"If you mean Pender, yes I have." He pulled a slip of paper from under his coat and shook it open. "Telegram here says he's berthed in Boston where he unloaded stores and waits to take on whatever cargo you have arranged." He handed the telegram to Grafton across the table and looked away. "It seems to me you've kept the Rip Tide out of this unsavory business with the Confederates and only risk my ship in your little venture."

Grafton looked up from the note. "This is not your ship, Captain Beckett," he reminded him. "This is my ship, and yes I want the Rip Tide to stay out of harm's way. Captain Pender will continue his profitable trade with the Union and we shall continue to take the risks." He cleared his throat. "Might I also remind you, Sir, that your own profit in this business has been substantial."

"So it has," Beckett started to apologize but a knock on the door brought the steward in with their supper. Grafton looked over the ship's log as he ate and the two men discussed the transfer of several

Wayne Vance

tons of cargo. Both agreed that the shorter time it spent on the dock, the better. Beckett was about to pour a second after dinner drink when they were again interrupted by a loud knock on the door.

"Enter!" Beckett shouted and saw a slightly shaken officer enter before him. He calmly looked the man over and took a sip of his drink before he asked. "Yes, what is it Mr. Hecker?"

"Captain, there is a full company of Union soldiers at the end of the pier and an Officer is headed this way. Sir, I believe they mean to board us."

Grafton remained seated, but he and Beckett exchanged glances. "Show that officer to my cabin, Mr Hecker." Beckett ordered.

"And, Mr. Hecker." Grafton cautioned. "Calm yourself."

Within five minutes Hecker was back with a Union Cavalry major at his side. "Major Bennett," he said, "may I present Captain Beckett of the Breakwater and its owner Captain Grafton also of the Bore Tide."

Beckett crossed the room and extended his hand in his usual jovial manner but Grafton did not get up, thereby making the Major come to him with a hand outstretched in friendship.

Again, Grafton did not rise. "Forgive me if I don't shake hands, Major." He stated with a deadly serious tone and stared harshly at the rather surprised officer, "until you declare the nature of your business on my ship."

"When I entered this room, I had rather thought Captain Beckett was the man in charge, as he looks more the part than you." He cleared his throat when Grafton did not react. "Beyond that he does not lack the manners of a gentleman or that of a good business man."

Grafton did not rise to the bait, but rather picked up his wine glass and took a sip while he continued to eye the officer. "What is it you want?" He sarcastically asked and set the glass down.

"Would you like a drink?" Beckett hurriedly offered from behind.

"Yes, thank you," he answered without averting his stare at Grafton. "Sherry if you have it."

Beckett poured the drink and offered it to Bennett before he sat down himself. "Won't you be seated now and tell us the nature of your visit to my ship?" He asked, as Grafton shot a glare at Beckett but said nothing.

"Well, gentlemen," Bennett began and took a seat on a wooden chair. "The Union needs your assistance in a matter of utmost importance. I have been instructed to present myself here and bring you," he looked directly at and raised his glass in Grafton's direction, "back to Washington City."

"I have no intention of going anywhere with you, Major," he sternly scoffed.

"Oh, I am sure I can change your mind," he smirked. "You see, I've brought an entire company of men with me to use if I have to."

Grafton leaned forward, "Useless," he smiled, "to you at least. Do you really think you have one chance in a million to get off my ship alive and give that order?" The comment caused Beckett to shift uncomfortably in his chair and scowl.

Grafton saw a concerned look descend on the Major's face, but he put up a good bluff when he replied, "I hope you are very good with that sword and pistol if that be your intention."

"I don't possess any scars if that's what you mean."

Bennett could see that his confrontation with Grafton was not going to net the results he wanted, so he changed tactics. "Look, gentlemen, perhaps we got off on the wrong foot here." He leaned forward and put his elbows on his knees while he spun the sherry glass in his fingers. "We really do need your help and I would appreciate it if you would accompany me by train to Washington. I assure you that you will be back in a few days and no worse for wear."

Grafton relaxed somewhat too and sat back, "Why don't you just tell us what this is all about."

"People of," he paused and looked to the ceiling. "People of a higher station will explain that as well as everything else," he smiled. "Anyway I don't know all of the details myself." He lied.

"And if I refuse?" Grafton countered.

Bennett drew a deep breath. "A ship which matches the description of the Bore Tide was seen by our navy six days ago entering the port of Richmond. She rode low in the water, and here you are today in New York, again low in the water." Bennett sat back up and smiled. "It is reasonable to assume, is it not, that you conduct business with the Confederate States using Union ports?"

"I am a Dutch business man exercising my rights to trade anywhere I deem prudent," he flatly retorted. "Besides, all the stores on my ship came from the West Indies, not Richmond."

"Perhaps, but not the stores aboard this ship and I rather doubt that Kingston needs those cannons and gunpowder to defend herself." He paused raising an eyebrow, "I am authorized to search all the contents of both ships." Bennett shook his head and leaned forward again with a smile. "Look, gentlemen, this is just idle speculation on both our parts. I am sure there will be no need for any un-pleasantries between us, because I know you will make the right decision in this matter."

Grafton picked up his glass and finished the contents before he roughly set the beaker back on the table, "what time does our train leave?" He asked with a smirk.

"Excellent," Bennett replied with a wide grin. "Our train departs at 11 tonight and we'll be in Washington tomorrow."

"Very well," Grafton nodded. "I'll meet you at the station a little before then."

Bennett rose with a concerned look on his face. "Don't disappoint me, Captain Grafton."

"I wouldn't dream of it, Major," he said sarcastically.

Captain Beckett crossed the room with the Major and pulled open the cabin door where Mr. Hecker stood just outside. "My first officer will show you back to the dock, Sir, and good evening to you."

Bennett stepped out through the hatch but turned to look back at Grafton. "Ten o'clock then," and disappeared with the deck officer.

Beckett shut the door and looked at his boss, "What do you make of all this?" He sounded very concerned.

"I don't know, but I sure as hell don't like it." He shook his head and looked down in thought, "and they're obviously on to us, that's for sure." Grafton sat in silent thought for a moment before he spoke. "Perhaps we'll have to start using an off shore port like Nassau to make the cargo trades from now on. That will add considerable sailing time to our routes," he sighed.

"If there is a next time," Beckett cautioned.

"While I am gone I want you to transfer all the cargo between the ships and make preparations for immediate departure."

"A great majority of my crew is still ashore Captain, and scattered around the city."

"Get them back as soon as you can and no one from the Bore leaves the ship." He rubbed his chin and considered his options. "Telegraph Captain Pender in the morning and tell him to load any profitable cargo he can muster and be ready to sail for Portsmouth on my orders. I may want him out of the Union States sooner than later." He stood up to leave but turned and pointed at the old captain. "You tell him to be prepared to pick up tradable goods over there for the southern markets."

"When do you really think you'll be back, Alexander?" Beckett asked with even more concern, "and what do you want me to do if you don't return?"

"Good question," he replied and raised an eyebrow with pause. "Stay in port until I do. If I am not back in a week, send out a party to ascertain my whereabouts and condition. If there are problems you can't control, act on your own instincts as to the safety of the ship, and if something really goes poorly, get out of here. I'll put Cole in command of the Bore Tide before I go and he can do the same." Grafton started out of the cabin but was stopped by Beckett's firm hand on his arm.

"I heard tell that the Union won a horrific battle with a tremendous loss of life somewhere near a place called Gettysburg just a few days ago. Word is it might even have changed the course of this war." The two men stared at each other for a moment. "Be careful out there Alexander," Beckett cautioned.

Grafton crossed the plank to his own command in the late evening hour and had the deck watch summon Mr. Cole to his cabin. He busily packed a few items into a travel bag when Cole knocked on his door. "Enter," he shouted and threw another pistol on the bunk next to his cloth bag.

"Deck watch said you wanted to speak with me Captain."

"Sit down, Bass, and pour yourself a drink," he motioned to the mess table where a decanter and glasses sat. "Pour me one as well."

Cole looked at the Captain's doings and asked with some concern, "are you planning on a trip?" He waved his hand toward the luggage, "or does this have something to do with those soldiers on the docks a little bit ago?"

"A little of both, I'm afraid."

Cole walked to the table, turned over two glasses and filled them with wine. "I had the men armed when we saw the Army appear. They stood out of sight to cut rope loose from the Breakwater if the situation turned sour, but I am afraid it would have been a futile effort with so little wind." He slid out a chair and sat down. An issue of arms to the crew was not protocol on any of Grafton's ships. That was unless approved by the Captain or they were going ashore on a raiding party.

Grafton finished with the bag and came to the table where he sat down across from his friend. "I am going to Washington tonight for what purpose isn't clear. A Major Bennett claims some important people there want our help and those troops were staged to prove the seriousness of the request." He picked up the glass for a drink and continued. "They know about our visits to Richmond and threatened to board the Breakwater to inspect her cargo if I didn't agree to go."

"What could be so important?"

"Whatever it is," he raised an eyebrow, "they are willing to overlook our clandestine trade for the assistance they seek."

Cole sensed that Grafton needed his help in this matter and asked. "What would you have me do, Captain?"

"I intend to put you in command of the Bore Tide until my return." He leaned on his forearms over the table toward Cole, "I want the men to stay on board, and no one leaves the ship." Beckett and I have agreed that he will send out a party and find the rest of his crew as well. We need to get our cargo unloaded and exchanged with him. When that task is complete, ready the Tide for sea," he sat back in silence for a moment then added. "You may have to beat a hasty retreat without me from this port."

Cole shifted in his chair. "The men aren't going to take that very well, Captain, they have looked forward to shore leave for some time now."

"Assemble them in the forward mess and I'll give them the bad news myself. Any man who elects to leave the ship before I return will be fired."

Knowing it was time to take his leave, Cole rose and started to the door but stopped and looked back to the table. "May I make a suggestion Captain?"

"Of course," he replied.

"Perhaps it would be wise to send Mr. Dobbs along with you, but at a distance and incognito like a shadow, as it were."

Grafton sat up and rubbed his left index finger along the line of his jaw in thought. "You know," he said after contemplation, "that's not a half bad idea. Send him up here to see me and let me know when the crew is assembled."

It only took a few minutes for Mr. Dobbs to appear and he was clearly nervous about being called to the Captain's berth. It was an event rare in nature. When he entered Grafton sized him up a moment before he spoke which only added to his second officer's stress. Jeffery Dobbs was a man in his early fifties with thick salt and pepper hair but because of the wrinkles around the eyes, he could easily be mistaken for much older. Grafton assumed the full beard covered even an older look to his face.

"You wanted to see me, Captain?"

"Sit down, Mr. Dobbs."

The man took a seat across from Grafton but stayed back from the table. He took off his hat and held it between his knees. He dressed exactly like Mr. Cole which wasn't a problem until now.

"I have a most important task for you tonight. You need to get out of those clothes and into apparel that will make you look like a commoner of the city." Grafton reached into his pocket and flipped a twenty dollar gold piece to him. Buy yourself a ticket on the late night train to Washington and have Mr. Cole issue you a side arm."

"What is it you want me to do in Washington, Sir?" he asked, rather confused, while he stared at the gold piece in his palm.

"In a few minutes I'll address the crew and then head for the train depot where I'll meet a Union Major. I want you to follow us, but at a distance and do nothing. Blend into the background, Jeffery, and keep an eye on things for me."

"Is that all, Sir?"

"It is hard to say where he'll take me and you may not be able to follow everywhere but you can determine if I get into trouble. If that happens, you get back here to Mr. Cole immediately." He paused and stared at the older man. "Can you do that Mr. Dobbs?"

Relieved that he was not in some kind of trouble, Dobbs smiled broadly and nodded, "Yes, Sir."

"Good man. Get cracking then."

Mr. Cole appeared at the door to advise the Captain that the crew waited in the forward mess. The two men walked together toward the mess but as they entered the room several of the men grumbled about being stuck on board ship.

"Is it true what Mr. Cole says about your decision to make us stay aboard ship, Captain?" someone shouted from the back of the room.

Grafton pulled a chair from under the table and stood on it. "Anyone who wishes to leave the ship may do so now. Just see Mr. Cole about your bounty share and he'll pay you off. If you do leave, don't ever come back to one of my ships again."

"We just want to know what's going on, Sir?" a man seated across the table asked with a whine.

"The reason I want you all to stay on board, Hopson," he said and looked down at him, "is because I'm not sure what is going on." He looked back up and around the room. "I want you men to keep this in mind; we are mostly Dutch, in a foreign country which is at war with itself, and we are doing business with a very unpopular government to the south. They have the capability to run us down whether it is here or on the high seas, to confiscate our cargo or even hang us. Until I know for sure what it is they require, I intend to look to the best interest of my ships and crew." The room was silent and he paused. "You'll just have to trust me on this for a few days."

"We're with you, Captain!" Someone shouted in the back and the rest of the room came to a roar of support.

"Good, that's very good. Now get your jobs done and I should be back in a few days. In the meantime, Mr. Cole is acting Captain." Grafton stepped down from the chair where several crewmembers slapped him on the back before he left the room.

Grafton stood quietly on the deck with Mr. Cole in the dark and covered some last minute details. Dobbs appeared dressed in some shabby dark clothing and wore an overcoat. He looked him up and down for a moment without saying anything.

"I am ready anytime you are, Captain, and will follow you at some distance."

Cole and Grafton shook hands before he left without saying a word to Mr. Dobbs. They watched together as Grafton disappeared down the wooden pier. "Look out for him, Mr. Dobbs, and mind your surroundings." Cole cautioned and then patted him on the shoulder before he gently pushed him toward the gang plank to begin his journey.

Grafton walked for a short time and decided to cut through a darkened alley between some tall brick buildings. At the far end he knew there were usually carriages on the brightly gas lit streets and from there he could summon a taxi to the rail station.

"Will you look at this dandy, Max." The voice in the dark momentarily startled Grafton and then two men appeared out of the night. Both were holding knives outstretched in their hands. A third voice from the shadows told the others he fancied the dagger sticking out of his red sash.

Suddenly the unseen man stepped between the other two, close enough, at least, for Grafton to see him. He was a man huge in stature, shabbily dressed with a distasteful odor about him. "Why don't you just hand over that there knife," he pointed, "and custom gun, sonny, so we don't have to carve you into little pieces," he growled.

Without saying a word, Grafton dropped his cloth bag. He kept his eyes on the larger man but in one movement threw the dagger from his sash. It stuck nearly to the hilt in the man's throat on his left. The other two men jerked in reaction from surprise and when they did, Grafton pulled out his saber in a blindingly quick move, swung it from his belt and instantly cut off three fingers of the man on his right. The inept robber screamed out in agony before he dropped his knife and fell to his knees crying.

The steel blade arced around and the very tip touched up against the center man's chin. An ever so small trickle of blood ran down the shining metal as it gently pressed into the flesh of his square jaw. "If you'd like to pick up my knife, I'll see you get a little something extra for your trouble," Grafton smiled.

The weary thief shook his head in the negative and took a half step back.

"Then why don't you collect your bloody friend there and get your asses out of my sight." The man readily agreed with a nod and Grafton watched while the two assassins stumbled and disappeared down the alley into the darkness. Just as they were going out of his sight, Mr. Dobbs ran past them toward him.

"Are you alright, Sir?" he asked excitedly and looked to see the last bit of life slip out of the man on the ground.

"No problems here, Mr. Dobbs."

"We've just started and I don't seem to be doing a very good job looking out for you," he apologized.

Grafton bent down and looked over the man he had just killed. He pulled the knife from his throat with a quick snap and looked back up at Dobbs. "You're doing exactly what I expect you to do." He wiped the blood from the blade on the dead man's pants and stood up. "Now, go buy your ticket and I'll see you on the train." The men parted and Dobbs hurried down the alley but looked back in silence at the surreal scene.

There was a distinct look of relief on Bennett's face when Grafton appeared on the depot's ramp as the train was about to leave the station without them. Bennett quickly introduced the lieutenant with him as James Overton, his aide, while they boarded. Grafton stepped from the platform and looked down the ramp where he saw Dobbs get on three cars down the line.

"You have berth seven down there," Overton pointed. "And we are in number twelve here." He quickly added. "We would like you to join us for a night cap in the dining car after you're settled.

Grafton opened the door to number seven and threw his bag into the berth. "I'm settled," he said. "I'll meet you in the dining car," and disappeared down the aisle. After a few minutes, the Major and his aide appeared for their nightcap, but by then Grafton had nearly finished his drink. Mr. Dobbs sat in an end booth at the back of the car reading a newspaper.

"Well, I see you didn't wait for us," the Major exclaimed before he took a seat across from Grafton. Lt. Overton slid into the booth and waved the porter over to their table.

The lieutenant shifted uncomfortably in his seat after he ordered drinks. "I don't want to seem impertinent, but if I didn't know better, Mr. Grafton, by your dress and arms, one could easily mistake you for some kind of pirate."

"I suppose there are those who are unfair minded, of course, in your government that would agree with you on that count." He took the last sip of his drink. "It does beg the question as to why they would want to summons such a man to council." He looked directly at the lieutenant and changed the subject. "You look old for a lieutenant." Grafton quizzed.

His face reddened, "I was a sergeant who won a field commission for gallantry and I surely wouldn't know the answer to your other question." He stammered.

"Mr. Grafton here is a curious and perhaps even a slightly worried man, Lieutenant Overton." Bennett informed him with a contemptible smile. "As should anyone be who deals with the enemies of the United States." He took a slow drink and eyed Grafton before he set the cup down, "but don't fear Sir, your questions will all be answered tomorrow."

Grafton's eyes flashed at Bennett and instantly became cold and piercing. "Don't misunderstand caution for fear, Major. Besides, I was under the impression that you are all Americans." He rose and dropped several coins on the table. "Until tomorrow then gentlemen," he said and walked away.

CHAPTER II
A MONETARY PROBLEM

Captain Grafton ate a hearty breakfast aboard the train before they arrived in Washington a little before nine. Several years had passed since he had been afforded the opportunity to visit the city and much had changed. It now more resembled a fortress garrison than that of a major metropolitan area of its time.

He watched as thousands of blue coated armed soldiers roamed the mostly dirty gravel streets and saw horse dung scattered everywhere. Wagons laden with all manner of supplies waited in long lines by the rail station while dust and wood smoke choked the still morning air. There was a flavor of excitement and intrigue about the place and most of the important people of the time resided here.

Major Bennett hailed a carriage and the three men made their way from the train depot toward Pennsylvania Avenue. Grafton did not notice Dobbs in the crowd, but assumed he lurked about and kept an ever vigilant eye on his duty.

Their carriage ride was of short duration. Grafton stepped out onto the wooden sidewalk and looked about to his surrounding, all of which bustled with activity. They were in front of a three-story drab stucco building with several tall pillars and four armed guards stood on post at the door. A large stone was engraved above the entrance which read, "War Department of the United States of America."

Grafton waited on the sidewalk with Lt. Overton while the Major paid the driver. Several enlisted soldiers passed him and turned at the sight of such a strangely outfitted man in their midst. He paid them no mind and kept his eyes roving the area until he spotted the person he was looking for. At last, he saw Mr. Dobbs across the dirty street leaning on a telegraph pole with a rather disconcerted look about him.

Lt. Overton watched the Captain intently and thought he had very busy eyes. They appeared like little mirrors which seemed to soak in everything and he felt this man carried a dangerous air about him. It clung to him like an aroma of death for anyone who dared cross him. The Lieutenant was just a bit in awe of this man because his demeanor had a solitary and singular presence one rarely sees.

"Seems we have arrived safely after all, Captain Grafton," the Major smiled. He stopped and bent backwards to look up at the inscription over the door before he gestured the others to precede him through the front arches. While they made their way to a second floor office, Grafton thought everyone in the hallways were in a hurry to get somewhere and nowhere at the same time.

The inscribed glass on the door Bennett opened for them read, "Office of the Under Secretary of War." Here again were armed soldiers on guard out front and they gave Grafton a once-over look.

It was a large room full of desks with soldiers who busily shuffled papers everywhere. They walked up to a desk in front of another interior door where a full Colonel sat and read documents. The background noise in the room stopped when Grafton entered except for a telegrapher in the far corner who banged away at his key. Their interest was piqued because no one else in the office was armed save the Marines out front.

The Colonel looked up from his papers at the men, especially eyeing Grafton. His eyes slowly roamed up and down his attire until they came to rest on the jewel-studded dagger in his sash. "Major Bennett, Lt. Overton and guest to see Mr. Nathan Stepp. I believe we are expected," he added and snapped his heels while he came to attention with a slight bow.

"This man will leave all his weapons with me before you go in," the Colonel waved his finger across the belt of Grafton.

"Not likely," Grafton replied, while all emotion drained from his eyes. He could physically see a chill come over the Colonel when their eyes met and he knew he had intimidated the older man with the short comment.

Bennett cleared his throat. "Ah, that will not be necessary in this case Colonel, I assure you."

"It's against protocol, Major, and you know it," he stubbornly insisted.

"Major," Grafton said and looked away from the Colonel. "It appears this trip and our meeting has concluded." He turned to leave, but Bennett's voice stopped him.

"Wait a minute, Captain, this is just a misunderstanding by the Colonel." The Major informed him. "I assure you it will be cleared up by Secretary Stepp and we will get this matter straightened out."

The Colonel placed both hands on the desk in front of his chair to help himself stand up. "Very well," he let out a sigh of disgust with the whole affair. "Wait here." He disappeared through the door and came back a moment later.

"The three of you may enter," he begrudgingly said and held the door open for them to pass.

It was a large beautiful office with pictures and flags hung on the walls. A huge wooden desk took up most of the back wall with several chairs in a semi-circle out front on a Persian rug. A well stocked liquor cabinet was against the far wall with a large round conference table in front. Grafton admired the portrait of a lovely young woman over a settee in the back. Secretary Stepp sat behind the desk and several aides scurried about with papers for him to sign.

"Gentlemen," he smiled and stood from his seat to better look at Grafton. "You must be our famous sea Captain, Alexander Grafton," he marveled and reached out his hand in friendship.

Grafton shook his hand across the desk while he sized the man up. Stepp was approximately sixty, nearly bald except for the grey hair on his temples and he had a long neatly kept white beard. He held a Cuban cigar in his left hand and his teeth were stained yellow from the habit.

"I must say, Captain, you look exactly as I imagined you would for someone in your profession." He noticed Grafton stared at the picture over his shoulder and he cleared his throat. "My daughter, Sir," he said and looked back himself. "I am so pleased that you agreed to come here to Washington and speak with me today"

To Grafton's mind he was much too jovial for the occasion but perhaps it was well meant. "Mr. Secretary, I'm not even sure what I am doing here in the first place," he said and shot a stern glance to Bennett. "And in the second place, it was not entirely voluntary."

Stepp cleared his throat again with some embarrassment and looked about the room. "Would you gentlemen excuse us please while the Captain, Major and I conduct our meeting." He shot a knowing glance at Overton, "you too Lieutenant, if you please." He looked to the gentleman on his right and added, "Mr. Weatherby, please ensure that we are not disturbed for any reason, short of losing the war of course." He smiled.

They watched as all of the men were ushered out of the room and the last man closed the massive door behind him. "Please," Stepp gestured with his hand, "be seated, as this may take some time."

He and Bennett sat down while Stepp came around his desk and sat in a chair next to Grafton. He turned so they could speak face to face. "May I offer you a cigar or drink, Captain?"

"Neither thanks."

"Very well then, let us get to our business at hand." He looked apologetically at Grafton, "As I said, I'm afraid this may take some time so please bear with me Captain. Being at sea for long periods you may miss out on pieces of information and news of current events, but you must also hear things that we land locked bureaucrats do not. And the places you go," he smiled, waved his arm and shook his head. "Imagine Major, this man can go right into the jaws of our enemies with impunity. What a wonderful way to gather and collect information about so many things."

"Are you asking me to be an informant for the Union, Mr. Stepp?"

"Not at all my boy, but we too have our sources," he continued, "cadets, or should I call them by their proper name, spies. They garner many bits of detailed data that by themselves make little sense, but when taken as a whole become very interesting. One most important theme all this information points out is that the South is in the midst of an economic crisis. You, of all people, must realize that unless they manage to somehow shore up their currency, this ill advised secession of theirs will fail."

"That's a rather elementary conclusion, don't you think." Grafton interjected. "It shouldn't take a bunch of spies and bureaucrats to figure that out. Their script has been inflated for months and now it is nearly worthless. Hardly anyone will trade goods for it these days."

"You are rather candid, are you not, about your dealings with these rebels?"

Grafton tipped his head. "Why not, according to the Major here, you people know all about my business relations with the border states."

"Do you know anything of the First Presbyterian Church of

Richmond?" Stepp asked completely changing the subject.

"Not first hand, but I haven't sung any hymns recently either," he shrugged. "I do know it's in the middle of a cavalry garrison on the outskirts of the city and I've heard rumors it may be more than a church."

Stepp and Bennett exchanged glances not un-noticed by Grafton. "You are unusually well informed, Captain," Stepp paused. "But you are right, because in the basement of that church there is a guarded room filled with papers, papers which are important to the Confederacy, and now to the Union. It is a very secure and well guarded place."

"Why tell me this?" Grafton questioned.

"Hear me out, Mr. Grafton." Stepp held up his hand. "Make no mistake we are in this fight to win no matter what it takes. We will reestablish the Union and bring these damn rebels back under one flag. It will be done either by military force or by skullduggery to destroy their half-hearted economy so they can no longer do business with people like yourself." He leaned forward, "and seeing as how the former isn't going all that well, we are about to embark on the latter."

"It is rather a forgone conclusion, is it not, that everyone knows the Confederacy will collapse eventually because of the industrial strength of the Union?" Grafton commented.

"Yes, it is. Unfortunately, we underestimated the South's resolve at the beginning of this war and they have put up an excellent military defense, the outcome of which is far from being answered." He stood up and began pacing in front of the two men. "I do not want to make the same mistake about the resiliency of their economy or its stability. By coincidence, some luck and well placed informants, we know what they intend to do to shore it up." He stopped and looked at Grafton with some concern on his face.

"There is some risk for me, and you too, I might add, in what I am about to divulge. We may have to adopt other unpleasant measures if you will not cooperate after I impart the information."

Grafton's curiosity was definitely up as to what Stepp had in mind. "I guess we'll both have to risk it. As a foreign national, I'm not sure why you people think I really care about who wins this conflict."

"Come now, Mr. Grafton, we both know you'll do much better financially trading with a unified America than a divided one," Stepp retorted.

Grafton raised one eyebrow but did not respond.

Stepp took a deep breath. "Very well," he said and sat back down moving his chair closer to Grafton. "Some well placed southern gentlemen have managed to secure an agreement with elements within the French government to procure approximately 10 million dollars of gold bullion from South Africa. One of your colonies I believe," he added with some sarcasm. "We also believe that they will use it to mint gold coin pieces which would be universally accepted and financially sound. Enough small denomination coins circulated about over a period of time could possibly save their script currency and their cause."

"As you might imagine, Captain, this cargo is much too precious to attempt a run of our blockade against their ports. So they devised a scheme to send it via the Pacific coast off Baja California and trade in Old Mexico at a dirt water town named Bahio Kino. It is to be delivered by the French ship Paris De Sal." He paused to study Grafton who was already deep in thought. "Do you know the ship, Sir?"

"Yes, I do, it is a retired 76 gun frigate, but an old fashion square rigger."

"A Confederate General named Applegate will attach himself in the very near future to a Texas regiment in Austin. He will carry with him from Richmond the authorization papers for the transfer of the gold. His cavalry will meet the French and escort the shipment across northern Senora back into Texas and the southern states." Stepp sat up straighter in his chair.

"By my count, Mr. Secretary," Grafton said and looked up from the floor into his eyes. "That's about 10 tons or 20 thousand pounds. Using their best wagons, in sandy conditions it would take at least four, maybe six, plus the oxen and another 40 or so wagons in support. Say, sixty men at least to run the train and another 400 to 600 to guard it." He tipped his head, "a culled down brigade and monumental task at the very least."

"Never the less, that seems to be their plan. And for the time being those authorization papers are locked soundly in that church in Richmond. However," he cautioned, "in a very short time they will be given to General Applegate for his journey west."

"You seem very well informed about the inner workings of the Confederacy and this plan," Grafton queried.

"We have some very good sources in this case plus the added advantage of having arrested the coin engraver some weeks ago in New York State for conspiring with the enemy." Stepp shook his head. "We have just about everything, except a way to foil it."

He smiled, "I hit upon the idea to steal it at sea, but with our navy tied up on the blockade and not being at war with France," he opened his arms, "how could our nation possibly attack a sovereign French ship?" He lowered his head and raised his eyes. "That's when your name came up in our conversation as a man who might be," he paused, "willing to risk an adventure in this matter."

Grafton was visibly amused. "What would ever possess me to attack a 76 gun French frigate three times my size on the open sea with the Bore Tide's 12 guns?"

The expression on Stepps' face became deadly serious. "One hundred thousand dollars," he waited for a reaction but got none, "and the exclusive rights to trade in the West Indies with the Union after the war." He cleared his throat. "We, that is, I, Secretary Stanton and President Lincoln knew a man such as you would not risk anything on this adventure without proper compensation, so we thought we would make this endeavor worth your while.

"It is not as generous as you are making out Sir," Grafton protested. "Great risk demands great rewards, but in this case I do believe you are being marginally fair."

"You'll do it then?"

"I will need some time to think this matter through Mr. Stepp, and how, or if, it could even be accomplished. But it seems to me you are overlooking an easier alternative."

He looked harshly at the Major, "Have we missed something?"

"You could pay the French 12 million dollars not to deliver the gold." He smiled.

"That's out of the question Sir." Stepp growled.

"Do you have other information about this matter?" Grafton inquired. "Like maybe the dates when the troops will arrive in California or the ship will arrive from Africa? It might be helpful," he added with a bit of ridicule in his voice.

"We have been very busy in that department." The Secretary stood up and went behind his desk to pick up some well used papers. You would have until the first few weeks of November before that ship arrived in Baja. It would seem that everything will converge there at or about that time." He looked up from the papers, "so as you can see, Captain, a plan in this matter is most urgent if we are to act at all."

Grafton counted out the weeks on his fingers in silence while Stepp watched. He looked up. "Are you sure this General Applegate hasn't already left for his trip with the papers?"

"Our information says he departs next week on the 15th." Bennett interjected.

"That's cutting it a little fine, don't you think?" Grafton asked. "Where did you get that information?"

"One of our aides has an academy mate set to travel with the General. It was he who passed on the information quite by accident."

Grafton stood and looked at the Secretary, "I believe I will take a stroll about your city for a few hours and look over its offerings."

"I'll accompany you, Sir." Major Bennett declared and rose to his feet.

"No, you will not, Sir." Grafton turned. "I need some time to think these things out and if you have me followed I will not cooperate in any scheme." He looked back at the Secretary. "Is that understood?"

"I give you my word you will not be molested by anyone from this office," he replied. "Captain Grafton," Stepp's voice stopped him. "We are having a small party at my home this evening if you would care to attend."

"Normally, I would be delighted but not tonight, thank you," Grafton nodded. He turned and walked out the door. This caused the Colonel at the front desk to immediately come in. "Is everything all right here?"

"Fine Colonel," Stepp answered. "Would you be so kind as to give us another minute or two."

When he left, Bennett turned back to the Secretary with a look of shock on his face. "Do you really think that was such a good idea? I mean to let him go like that with the information you gave him."

"Not especially, but at some point we will have to give him a long leash," he sat back down in his chair. "The man's a pirate and profiteer, and I'd venture not very trustworthy, but we do need him. Unfortunately," he scowled, raised an eyebrow and mumbled. After some reflection he looked directly at Bennett. "Whatever plan he comes up with, you and some others are going along to see he doesn't get lost."

"You really think he'll be back?"

"Oh, yes, he'll be back. There is no way he would let 10 million slip through his hands."

"You mean one hundred thousand don't you, Mr. Stepp."

Stepp dropped his pen on the desk, removed the cigar from his clenched teeth and sat back, "I believe Captain Grafton thinks in larger numbers, Major, and if we do not remain vigilant he would take it all."

The July heat was intense out on the street when Captain Grafton emerged from the federal building. Mr. Dobbs, who had been leaning against a light post across the street nearly asleep, suddenly stood up straight when he saw his boss. They exchanged glances before Grafton started off down the wooden sidewalk. Dobbs shadowed him and followed along on his side of the avenue until Grafton turned down a quiet lonely alley.

Dobbs stopped and watched to be sure no one followed his boss and he looked suspiciously at everyone moving up and down the busy street. Finally, after several minutes he crossed over to the alley and cautiously moved along the same path as Grafton. It was only about four feet wide and cooler in the long shadows of the tall buildings on each side. Halfway through, Grafton stepped out from behind some crates and startled Dobbs.

"I'm glad to see you are being careful, Mr. Dobbs."

"Gees, Captain you nearly scared the life out of me, Sir." Dobbs gasped.

Grafton smiled for a moment at the older man's distress. "Your task here is finished Mr. Dobbs. I want you to get back to the ship and tell Mr. Cole everything is fine. Have him continue to transfer our cargo with the Breakwater but also tell him to leave some room for additional stores. After the Breakwater is loaded make sure they both sit tight, but I want them ready for sea. I will follow you back in a couple of days."

"All right, Captain," Dobbs answered somewhat confused. "Are you sure you will be safe here?"

"I am fine Mr. Dobbs." He looked around for any unwanted eyes and seeing none, he gently pushed the older man's arm, "be on your way now."

After he watched Dobbs leave the alley, Grafton began a leisurely walk about town and took in the sights of the bustling capital. However, his mind was totally preoccupied with the task at hand while he worked out a time table for success. Eventually he came upon a pub which also served meals.

Grafton took up a table in the back and spent the next several hours calculating the skills, equipment and people he would require for his scheme to pan out. He also calculated his odds for victory in this matter, and they were not good.

Later that afternoon, he made his way back to the Secretary's office where he was warmly welcomed by Mr. Stepp. The three men sat down around the big conference table, to enjoy some Port and discuss his plan of action.

CHAPTER III
THE PLAN

The late afternoon sun cast beams through the massive office windows which cut the smoke in the room and made everything glow orange, silhouetting the large draped American flag on the wall. Captain Grafton sat back in his chair and began to lay out his plan for the Secretary and Major Bennett.

"Mr. Stepp you say that you want to deny the South the use of this gold for the recovery of their script, but it seems to matter little as to its disposition. Frankly, I find it hard to believe you mean to give me a carte-blanche commission to sink and plunder a French frigate."

The Secretary raised an eyebrow and knew his benefactor was about to propose a theft of the bounty.

"I see the situation somewhat differently, gentlemen. You need not only sabotage their economy by depriving them of this gold, but rather you should also put it to good use against them. That's very hard to do if your intention is merely to send it to the bottom."

"The general idea from the start, Captain, was to send it to the deeps, because it couldn't reasonably be taken by forces on land. Given the vastness of the region they have to transport it across, the fact it will always be in Mexico or deep in the Confederacy has ruled that option out." Major Bennett interjected sarcastically.

Grafton turned his head toward Bennett. "I do not believe Mr. Stepp here shares your enthusiasm for sending his treasure to the bottom, or he would not have mentioned the authorization papers located in the church of Richmond." He looked back at Stepp before he smiled. "You want it for yourself."

Stepp cleared his throat. "Nonsense," he retorted, "I want it for the Union." He raised an eyebrow, "And why not? We could, as you suggest Captain, put it to much better use than those troublesome rebels. And it would teach those damn French a lesson not to meddle into our affairs."

"Are we agreed then, gentlemen, that our goal here is to steal the property of the Confederate States?" Grafton asked.

Stepp gently nodded his head in the affirmative while Bennett carefully studied the Captain in silence. Finally at length he asked.

"You have some sort of scheme, I suppose, to make this miracle happen?"

"Indeed I do, Major, but I'll need the help of some very special men and rather exotic equipment." He looked to the Secretary, "and it will take your powers to find and retain them."

"What is it you require, Captain?" Stepp slid forward and eagerly asked, excited now by the prospects of the chance to grab the gold instead of lose it to the sea.

"Do you happen to know a Colonel by the name of Jefferson Langston?" Grafton queried.

"Why yes, I do, Captain," Bennett quickly answered. "He was a fine officer with General Bufford's 3rd Corp Cavalry in the Army of the Potomac and quite possibly the best swordsman in the entire army."

"Was, you say?" Grafton raised his eyebrows.

"That's right. Unfortunately, he was killed not far from here on the first day of battle at a place called Gettysburg."

"He was a gallant Northern officer who resisted siding with his southern countrymen." Stepp added.

"Hardly," Grafton snorted.

"Just what do you mean by that remark?" Bennett challengingly asked. "Explain yourself, Sir."

"Calm down Major." The Secretary cautioned.

"The good Colonel is, or rather was," Grafton looked over at Bennett, "a southern sympathizer and true to Virginia."

Bennett started to protest but thought better of it when Grafton continued.

"His plantation is on the James River and he intended to be in the Northern army when it invaded his country and thereby save his interests." Grafton turned back toward Stepp and shrugged. "He was hedging on one of his bets, that the South might lose the war." He paused and asked rhetorically. "What better position to be in when the enemy army marches into your backyard than at the head of the column? And if the South were to win, his elderly father lives on the property, being protected by Jefferson's loyal servant, Nelson Black."

"How is it that you are so well informed about this man?" Stepp asked with curiosity.

"That is a long story, Mr. Secretary, but by coincidence Nelson

Black is the man I will need to help recover those papers in Richmond." Grafton could see Stepp was not satisfied and still looked for an explanation about his recent knowledge.

"In 1846, I was a lad of fifteen on board my father's ship, the Rip Tide. We were trading around the Orient and sailed back and forth to the west coast of America. It is where I learned my skills of the sea."

"We lay in at Kyoto Japan one April morning to pick up some cargo which wasn't much appreciated by the Japanese government, so our stay was to be brief. Traditionally, they were not friendly to outsiders, but our Dutch counterparts had made some in roads so we and other ships took advantage of a short lived lucrative situation." He took a drink of port then started rolling the glass in his hand and thought of his past.

"We were about to weigh anchor in the misty morning air on the high tide when we were approached by a long boat. Two men came aboard that morning, one was Jefferson Langston and the other was his slave, Nelson Black. For a young and impressionable boy, he was a sight to behold."

"How so?" the Major asked.

"Imagine if you would an Arabian Knight. He was huge, possibly the largest man I had ever seen, at least six feet four inches and massively built to boot. He wore a wrap or turban on his head which made him look like a giant and his body was rippled with muscle. His white shirt and pants were made of sailcloth and he was barefooted. Very plain, save for one fact."

"Which was?" Stepp interjected.

"He wore a red sash on his waist with two swords, one of which was the most beautiful Kamato Samurai fighting blade you would ever see. It was deeply engraved with an ivory handle and had a hand made gold and leather sheath about 32 inches long. His short backup dagger was identical in structure and stuck out under the sash. I had only heard slaves mumble or talk in some guttural gibberish which made his speech a real surprise. His voice was deep and clear, with an unmistakable upper class British Empire accent."

"You say this man lives in Richmond, guarding Langston's father?" Stepp asked almost in disbelief.

"I spoke with him just last month." Grafton informed him.

"Naturally he doesn't look the same given his location and the fact he must play the part of a downtrodden black slave. He rarely if ever speaks, but mark my words, he is the same man I met all those years ago and then some."

"I have never heard of such a sword or the existence of a black English slave. And why would you have need for such a man on this mission?" Stepp insisted.

"He is, bar none, the best edged weapons, sword and knife man in this country and I will have need of him to quietly take the church in Richmond."

"A southern Negro slave you say. How can he be trusted?" Bennett scoffed.

"It was a long voyage from Japan around the Orient to San Francisco. Black didn't have to, but he befriended a young boy on that ship. He taught me many useful things about swordsmanship, honor, loyalty and duty, but more than that he taught me about judging men." Grafton nodded. "I trust him."

"How did this slave become so proficient with a sword?" Stepp wanted to know.

"Herman Langston had a rebellious son and decided to send Jefferson to Europe for some culture. A very young Nelson Black accompanied him to serve as a valet and in doing so he was exposed to the finer gentlemen of Britain and their language." Bennett looked somewhat confused and Grafton raised an eyebrow at him. "It's where his impeccable speech came from."

"Langston enjoyed and studied weapons of all kinds." Grafton continued. "Over time he became extremely proficient with both pistol and sword. He went to France to study under a master swordsmen and complete his skills. It was there he decided to teach his slave some of those skills so he might readily have a mentor to practice with in private. Nelson surprised and perhaps even somewhat frightened his master. You see, he was a much faster learner than Langston anticipated, and soon could best him with the blade."

Yes, but how in the world did they end up in Japan where you found them?" Stepp asked in some confusion.

"While in France, Jefferson heard rumors from Dutch traders that there was a cult in Japan called the Samurai who were the finest swordsmen in the entire world. They claimed these men had also mastered a physical fight style unmatched anywhere."

"The temptation for him to learn this art was too great of an opportunity to pass up. He and Nelson sailed for Japan, along with an English scribe who could speak that language. They eventually ended up in Kyoto where they found a willing Samurai master eager to teach his secrets. He considered himself to be a progressive man of his culture and wanted Europeans to open trade with his country."

"Unfortunately, after eighteen months or so, relations with the other Samurai in the area deteriorated." Grafton shrugged his shoulders. "They had a different point of view about outsiders, the results of which necessitated that Jefferson and Nelson flee for their lives. It was just by luck that we had happened to show up or they would have been executed."

"Perhaps, we know now a little of why you dress and act the way you do Captain?" Bennett coyly commented. "And carry that sword and dagger in that sash. Maybe you consider yourself in his league as a swordsman?"

Grafton shot back at Bennett with an annoying glance. "I am very good with my weapons Major, but to stand and live for more than a few seconds in a battle against Nelson Black would be an honor. He's capable of killing most any man he confronts in only fractions of a second, if he so chooses." A long silence fell over the room.

"Just how will you employ this slave's skill, Captain?" Stepp asked and broke the quiet with a change of subject.

"We must take the church and eliminate the guards without any shots before we access the safe. Nelson and I should be able to accomplish that." He cleared his throat. "That is where the second man I require comes in. He is one Albert Reynolds Martrovich."

"Are you sure this slave will help you in such a matter?" Stepp inquired.

"He is a slave, that is true enough, but he considers himself a free man and acts only out of loyalty to the younger Langston." He raised his brow. "The old man is deathly afraid of him. It should be no problem to purchase him over now that the son is dead. I have offered in the past to take him out of the south, but he will only go when he feels his debt to Jefferson has been paid." Grafton rubbed his fingers over his jaw in thought. At last he answered. "He'll help."

"And what about this man, Martrovich?"

"You will have to arrange his freedom from jail because, the last I heard, he was incarcerated in Upstate New York."

"For what, in God's sake?" Stepp asked shaking his head.

"Theft, safe cracking and forgery I would assume, if he has stayed true to his profession, that is."

"All right, let's say you've taken this church with your Negro and his weapons, and even managed to open the safe with your thief. Why all this trouble and what's next?" Bennett sounded impatient.

"We will take the authorization papers then return forgeries to the safe. We will also take any gold or money so the sheriff or Army guard will assume it is a robbery by a common thief. Obviously, only someone who didn't understand the importance of the papers would leave them behind." He curled his lip, "I doubt anyone has broken the wax seal on that document, so they should be easy to forge. In fact, the hard part will be duplicating the seal, but Martrovich should be up to that as well."

Stepp seemed impressed so far with the plan. "So, Captain, now that you have the real papers in your hands, what's next?" He asked.

"We sail for Baja around the Horn and arrive before the French. I estimate no more than seventy to eighty-five days sailing time. On arrival, I will put a party ashore disguised as Confederate soldiers and hide my ship. When the French show up, I will have the proper papers to get the gold and the wagons in which to transport it.

"Upon completion of the transfer and after the gold is ashore, I will let the frigate leave and place some French imposters as crew on the beach. They will impart a sad tale to the arriving Confederate General that the French ship went down from a pirate attack with most all hands." Grafton smiled.

"Clever," Stepp observed and leaned back in his chair. "What if General Applegate has the bad taste to arrive ahead of the French ship?"

"Then, Sir, I will take the frigate by force, steal the gold and send her to the bottom." Grafton sternly commented without feeling.

"A few hours ago you were in no hurry to confront a ship which out guns you almost ten to one." Bennett scoffed.

Grafton drew a deep breath. "As you might imagine, Mr. Stepp, in a case where I should endeavor to fight the French, I will again need your help."

"And that help would be?" Stepp asked.

"I will need four Gatling guns and forty thousand rounds of ammunition for each gun. Not the old style powder gun, mind you, I want the latest up-to-date model with the case round feed mechanism." Grafton insisted on the type of weapon, pointing his finger at the Secretary. "Additionally, I will need fifty repeater rifles with a thousand rounds each."

Secretary Stepp had a look of amazement on his face. "Where in the world did you come by the information that we have such weapons? That is brand new technology and very hard to get!" He almost stammered indignantly.

"The South has very good spies also, Mr. Stepp, and Confederate generals must talk about something at boring Richmond social parties. Besides," he paused, "difficult or not, to take ten million dollars of gold in wartime is not easy nor is it a mission for the faint of heart." Grafton stressed his demands. "Like it or not, I need the guns because without them, it's no deal."

Stepp leaned his elbows on the table, placed his forehead into his hands and thought about the requests. "You shall have your guns, Captain, if you can assure me this plan will work." He said and did not look up.

"It will all depend on timing, fair winds and luck." He smiled, "something I have always had in abundance.

"How long should it take before we know?" Stepp asked, with his head still down.

"I intend to have the Breakwater sail to Colon and stand by. We will transfer the gold overland from the Pacific to the Atlantic and sail for Washington, to arrive, I would hope, before Christmas." He paused, "Simple," Grafton shrugged. "But to make that transfer I desperately need a man by the name of Joseph Elder and four heavy load wagons."

"I take it this Elder is some kind of a teamster?" Stepp stated, looking up from his position.

"He is," Grafton replied.

Bennett, who had listened quietly, interrupted. "He is also a trouble maker and gunfighter of sorts, assigned as a scout with Meade's 1st New York. His reputation as a killer precedes him wherever he goes, Sir. Besides there is a railroad between Colon and Panama City, why not use it?"

"It's too dangerous and we can better protect it on the road. Having a gunfighter along on this trip isn't going to be a disadvantage either, Major." Grafton turned and quipped. "It is possible, however unlikely, that I could lose the Bore Tide to combat tactics and bad luck. In that case, we will have to move the gold overland through Confederate or Mexican territory and I, for one, wouldn't mind having him along."

"I've heard enough," Stepp interjected between the pair. "This plan is near lunacy Captain Grafton," he scoffed loudly than sat quietly for a moment before muttering under his breath. "Therefore, it just might work."

Stepp looked weary and tired from the long day. He took a deep breath, "I will put your proposal before the Secretary in the morning and we shall see if he is as crazy as you are, Sir." He rose up from his seat. "Do you have quarters here Captain Grafton?"

"No sir, I do not."

"See to it, Major, and make sure it is the finest we can offer." He picked up his satchel and headed for the door. "Good night, gentlemen, and I will be in touch very soon Mr. Grafton."

CHAPTER IV
PREPARATIONS

On the night of, but after their meeting with the Under Secretary of War, Captain Grafton got a glimpse of Major Bennett's shortcomings and loving mistress. In a word it wasn't who, but what - alcohol. The Major became visibly intoxicated in the lounge and was assisted from the table to his rooms by the hotel staff. Grafton instinctively knew this weakness could be exploited in the future, but it could also lend itself to be a fatal flaw in his plans. It was an addiction he would keep an eye on and, if possible, turn it to an advantage.

A young dispatch courier of 12 or 13 years, with blond hair curling out from under his bright new army cap, ran for all his worth between the bustle of carriages, horses and men on the street. He moved swiftly from the wooden sidewalks with fashionably dressed women to the dirty gravel street. His movement flowed with the rhythm of noises around him while he pushed forth on his errand. Clutched tightly in his small hand, he had a folded piece of paper with a red wax seal from the Secretary of War and the resolute look of determination on his face to reach his destination.

He burst through the door of the Imperial Hotel, only to be confronted by the large burly doorman who grabbed him by the collar and pulled him around in his tracks. "Hold on there, boy. Just where do you think you're going in such a hell fired hurry?" He asked, bending down so his face was at the lad's level.

"Let me go!" He squealed loudly, squirming in the tight grip. "I got an important message for Captain Grafton from the government and they won't be very happy if you delay me."

"The government you say." He released his grip and the boy dropped back onto his heels. The big man smiled, "Well, I guess we mustn't keep the Captain waiting." His smile evaporated and his tone deepened. "Message or no, there'll be no running in here to disturb our guests boy," he pointed his fat index finger at him. "Do you understand me?"

The boy hung his head and looked at the paper in his hand, "Yes Sir."

"Then be on you way boy." He responded.

Grafton had just dressed and prepared to join the hung over Major in the dinning room for breakfast when he heard a soft knock on his door. He pulled it open and had to look down at the messenger. "What is it, lad?"

"I," he stammered at the sight of the man before him. "I got a message for you, Sir." His raised hand shook not knowing if this would-be pirate would slay him with his sword or shoot him with his pistol. Either way he was mightily afraid and at the same time, impressed with the man before him.

Grafton ripped off the wax seal. He read the message and looked down at the dispatch runner. "Wait right there." He walked over to his writing table where he leaned over and scratched out a short note then folded the paper in half.

Grafton returned to the doorway and reached into the top left side of his sash. He pulled out a silver dollar and flipped it to the boy. "Now, see this telegram gets sent out immediately and when it does I want you to find me over at the War Department and tell me so. Understand?"

The boy snatched the money out of the air and turned as he ran toward the stairs looking back over his shoulder. "Thank you, Sir," he said with a big smile and skipped a step. "I'll see it gets sent."

Grafton was amazed when he found a fully recovered Major Bennett in the dining room. The depth of his tolerance for alcohol was impressive, especially at this early hour. He nursed a glass of Bourbon for his morning meal. Grafton set down across from him and pulled the cloth napkin from the table and shook it out to place on his lap. The waiter immediately approached and took his order for bacon and eggs.

"Well, Major," he began, "seems I have good news this morning," he paused. "We are to meet with Mr. Stepp at 10AM for the finalization of my plan."

"That certainly didn't take long." he casually observed. "I would say the Under Secretary was up all night to convince his superiors to place their trust in his mysterious privateer."

Grafton let the remark pass and several seconds of silence hung between the men while he sipped on his coffee and eyed the Major. "I wonder," the Major finally said, thinking out loud, "how he proposed to rein you in on such a lucrative mission, and keep you from stealing all the money?" He looked up at Grafton and raised an eyebrow.

The waiter stepped up between the two men and set Grafton's breakfast on the table. When he stepped away, Grafton picked up his utensils and began to cut the eggs. "I suspect he will want you and some of your men to accompany me." He shrugged his shoulders, "It makes no difference to me. If we strike a bargain for the one hundred thousand dollars, he has no fear." Grafton glared at the Major, "I do not usually cross people on contracts once I agree to them."

"Yes," the Major countered and leaned forward with a glare. "But exactly how long has it been since you had ten million dollars in the pot, or for that matter, in the hold of your ship?" he asked rhetorically.

Grafton smiled deviously. "It does rather up the ante."

The two men caught a carriage out in front of the hotel after breakfast and went directly to the War Department. Mr. Stepp waited there with Lieutenant Overton in his office and it did seem, by his appearance, that the Major was right about him being up all night.

"Gentlemen." The Secretary smiled and stood when they came in. "Please be seated," he waved his arms to the chairs in front of his desk. "We have a great many matters to discuss."

Both men took a chair and watched while Stepp lit up a rather large cigar, then offered one to his guests from the beautifully carved wooden box on his desk. The Major leaned forward to remove one before he sat back and lit it. Grafton raised his hand in a quiet polite refusal and his eyes followed Overton out of the room.

"I took your proposal to Secretary Stanton and he relayed it directly to the President, Mr. Grafton. I must say both men are not impressed with your odds for success. Nor, I must confess, are they sure about your loyalty to this project." He raised his arm to silence Grafton before he had a chance to protest. "Oh, it's not about your character," he lied. "But rather more about your business practices with the South and the fact that you're not an American citizen.

He cleared his throat, "I was able, however, to convince them that those shortcomings are the exact reasons why you are undoubtedly the most qualified man for the job."

"I take it then that we have an accord?" Grafton asked.

"Yes, but I'm afraid it comes with some stipulations." He

answered.

"What is it they want for their hundred thousand dollars, Mr. Secretary?"

Stepp stood up to think before he answered and paced about his desk with his hands behind his back, puffing on his cigar. At last he stopped and looked directly at Grafton. "This mission will not take place unless you agree to these demands. You see, they come directly from the President." He pointed the wet end of his cigar at him to emphasize the importance of the requests.

Grafton glanced over at Bennett and knew his attendance would be part of the deal. "You'll have all the equipment and supplies you requested and my people are searching for the men you named as we speak." He sat back down and stared at Grafton. "You will take Major Bennett and ten of his men along."

"For what?" he growled, "To keep me in line?" he asked sarcastically and raised an eyebrow. Grafton thought about it for a second before he added, "I won't have it!" he exclaimed. "Bennett maybe," he conceded, "but not his men. The last thing I need is a bunch of seasick soldiers aboard who will eat up all our supplies for no good purpose."

Stepp let the refusal and confrontation pass for the moment. "Alright, as long as Bennett here goes along. Besides, the President has a much better argument to keep you on our side in this matter." He opened a file on his desk and took out a paper. "I have here a presidential commission which makes you a full colonel in the Army of the Potomac. It places you in command of all operations in regards to this mission."

Major Bennett's jaw dropped and his mouth opened. "Sir, you can't be serious with this nonsense?"

"Quite the contrary, Major," Stepp grinned. "This document will do more to keep Captain Grafton's loyalty than any ten men ever could." He handed it to Grafton to read while he looked at Bennett. "You see, Major, if he should decide to betray us in this matter it would be considered treason and he could be hung." His stare returned to Grafton. "Surely, Captain, you can't expect the President to not have some power over you and the outcome here?"

Grafton finished the letter and smiled, handing it back to Stepp.

"Tell your President that I would be honored to accept a commission in his army for the purpose of this mission, as long as my men are not being drafted as well."

"I think your commitment will be sufficient in this undertaking Captain, besides," Stepp pointed out. "Maritime law will be in effect on the seas in regards to your crew, and this army commission will give you certain advantages should you find yourself boarded or caught on land."

"I hope you realize, Mr. Stepp, that events may intervene or over-take us in the next few months. That may mean I have to adapt my movements or strategy not in accord with some people." Grafton commented, then looked at Bennett.

The Secretary took a deep breath and sighed. "Once you walk out that door, Sir, it's like I have shot a bullet out of a gun and there is no way to bring it back. The events we set in motion here today will be hampered by a lack of communication between us." He crossed his arms over his desk. "You must use your best judgment and proceed as you see fit, Colonel, but remember the outcome of your actions will define you for the future, Sir."

Grafton and Bennett got up to leave but were stopped by Stepp's voice. "The President will deny he knows anything about the destruction of French property or an attack on French shipping in the Pacific. You do not have his permission to do so and should it occur that you lose, you are on your own in that matter." He smiled. "Is that clear?"

"Abundantly," Grafton replied. "If I am extremely lucky I may not have to destroy anyone."

"Good! Your equipment is already on its way to New York. See to it that you sail at your earliest convenience." Stepp stood up, with a worried look on his face. "I wish the best to you and your gallant crew, Captain." He looked down again and mumbled, "And good luck, Sir."

Grafton and Bennett stood on the outside steps of the War Department to wait on a carriage. "Looks like you will be a guest aboard my ship for several months and I hope you are ready to take orders from a privateer." The Major had a distasteful look on his face. "Why Major," Grafton smiled, "I believe you are already seasick." His smile faded when he looked up to see the young messenger boy running toward him on the street.

He came up to them out of breath. "All done, Sir, it was sent an hour ago."

Grafton held out his hand and they shook. In doing so, he slid another dollar into his palm. "Good lad." He nodded. A carriage pulled up and the two men climbed aboard. The boy slammed the door shut and turned the dollar in his hand while he watched the wagon disappear down the street.

"What message?" Bennett asked, but Grafton ignored him to watch the city pass by outside the carriage.

It was almost dark when a man with grey hair and a mustache stood up from the deck to wrap a dark brown rope from hand to elbow. He looked much older than his actual years and when he smiled, the lines under his eyes deepened. "Pass the word to Mr. Cole, Haskell, the Captain's back."

The sailor nodded in the direction of the pier and when Haskell turned his head he could also see his commander walk toward them with another man. He dropped his mop and looked back at VanDorn before he ran aft.

"Captain's back, Sir!" He shouted up to the poop deck and pointed over the port rail.

Cole's eyes looked along his arm to the dock and he smiled. "Very good Haskell," he replied. Cole walked over to the rail and bowed his head in relief.

Grafton and Bennett came up the gang plank of the Breakwater to the deck. "Permission to come aboard," Grafton said.

"Granted, Captain, and welcome back, Sir."

"Thank you, Mr. Hecker." Grafton nodded. "Would you please inform Captain Beckett I would like him to join us aboard the Tide." The second officer tipped his hat and left toward the Captain's quarters. Grafton and Bennett crossed over to the Bore Tide and to Mr. Cole, where he made introductions.

Grafton was again comfortable in his own world. His steward had provided a hot meal for the men in the officers' mess. Over dinner, Captain Beckett told him all the cargo had been transferred in both ships and he was ready to sail. With dinner over, they settled in for drinks and a strategy talk. Grafton laid out only the basic elements of his plan, especially leaving out the part about the Richmond church and their conversations with the Under Secretary. The others quietly listened to his presentation until he asked them what they thought.

"That's a lot of money, Alexander. Are you sure the South will let you take it so easily?" Beckett asked. "And what about the men, how will you get them to cooperate in such a dangerous undertaking? Some of them are sure to be killed, perhaps, even yourself."

"The usual way, Captain Beckett," he smiled, "money." The others remained silent and reflective. "I'll provide you the specific details when and as you need them."

"What, exactly, is it that you need me to do?" Beckett asked as Grafton stood with one foot up on a chair and pen in hand over a world map which lay over the table. He dropped the pen and looked to Beckett.

"I want you to sail tonight on the late tide for England. Unload and sell your cargo, then make way to Colon on the Isthmus of Panama. Also, if he gives you any trouble, tell Mr. Cripps, at the Portsmouth office that you sail under my orders. I want you there before the last day of November and with an empty cargo hold. You will stand by until you hear from me."

"And what if I don't," he paused and swallowed. "Hear from you?"

Grafton looked up and around the table at the others. "Stay until Christmas," he advised. "If we're not there by then, we're all dead." He let the long silence speak for itself and after a moment he looked at his second in command. "Mr. Cole, have the hands prepare to move the ship so Captain Beckett can depart and we will re-dock. What time is the high tide?"

Beckett again cleared his throat and took out his pocket watch, "One AM I believe."

"Very well then," Grafton looked around at the men one more time. "After we are secure, Mr. Cole, you can let our men go on shore leave, but I want them back by 1300 hours day after tomorrow. Any man not back by then is not to be allowed back on the ship. Make that abundantly clear to them, Sir." The men shook hands and took a moment for goodbyes before they parted.

"Major, I will quarter you with Mr. Cole and have your baggage delivered there. You of course are free to leave the ship if you wish but the same rule applies about being back here." Grafton smiled. The men ushered out, with Mr. Cole in the rear. Grafton's voice stopped him and he turned before he stepped through the door. The Captain studied his map and did not look up. "Send my steward in to clean up this mess. And Mr. Cole," he added. "Short of being attacked by Confederates or the ship sinking, I do not wish to be disturbed for the rest of the night.

Mr. Cole smiled and nodded. "I'll see to it, Sir."

The Breakwater had sailed and the Bore Tide was now tied directly to the pier. Captain Grafton had finally gotten a good night sleep and quietly came up on deck in the early morning light. A thin mist hung low over the harbor and a blue-red sky with light streaks beamed through the haze. It was a beautiful crisp July morning. He could see that his second officer stood ahead of him and fought off sleep before his watch ended.

"Good morning, Mr. Dobbs!" The Captain smartly announced.

Dobbs nearly jumped out of his skin by the surprise voice and suddenly became erect. "Yes Sir, that it is, Sir. He clasped his hands behind his back and looked toward the bow trying to compose himself. "Glad to see you back safe on board Sir"

"How many of the crew is still on board, Mr. Dobbs?"

"Twelve I believe sir."

"Good. Sometime later today we should receive some government cargo in crates and boxes." The Captain stepped up next to Mr. Dobbs. "There will be four heavy load wagons as well. When they arrive I want the crates loaded first. Whatever labels they have, remove them. Mark them as ships stores or whatever you want."

"I'll see to it, Sir."

"There is more, Mr. Dobbs." Grafton interjected. "I want you to remove the wheels from the wagons so we can stack them on top of those crates. I want it so it would be the very devil to open them up for inspection. Put everything in the forward hold so it doesn't interfere with the unloading of the rest of the cargo in Richmond."

"We won't be unloading them with the rest of stores I take it?" Mr. Dobbs asked.

"No, we will not."

"May I ask what is in the crates, Sir?"

"Equipment," Grafton smiled, "for a special purpose. I will be going ashore and should return before dinner. Tell Mr. Cole he has the ship."

"Yes, Sir," Dobbs replied and watched the Captain walk toward the gang way and down onto the pier.

Grafton made his way on foot to the center of the business district and watched the sleepy city awake. He stopped for breakfast and coffee at a sidewalk café and relaxed there until about nine. He went to a map makers store located on Broadway where the sign over the door was marked, "The Old Cartography Shoppe." When Grafton pushed open the door a tiny bell on a spring above began to softly clang. The shop was a quiet place, much like a library, with maps everywhere all stuffed into cubby holes along the walls. A silver-haired old man with spectacles came out of a back room and smiled when he saw his customer.

"Captain Grafton!" He exclaimed in a soft frail voice. "It has been such a long time since you visited my shop and I am so glad to see you again."

"As always, Mr. Lausar, I am glad to see you as well." He waved his hand over toward the maps behind the counter. "And as usual, I see you have a grand selection of charts."

"Where would you be off to this time, Captain?" he smiled.

"Baja," Grafton whispered. "We'll be going around the Horn so I will also need current maps of that and of Drake's Passages. Additionally, I will require anything you may have around the area of the Panama Isthmus."

"I am confident I can assist you on all counts, Captain Grafton." he answered and turned to survey his supply. The Captain watched him slide a step stool in front of the cabinets and, with sore joints, slowly climb up the steps to pull the maps out of their slots. He managed to get everything down, then rolled the charts together and slid them into a fine leather case. "Is there anything else you'll need for your journey?"

Grafton set payment on the counter and picked up the leather bound scroll of maps. He smiled, "A great deal of luck if you have any of that." He went to the door and pulled it open. Again the little bell quietly chimed.

"I hope you will fare well Captain," the old man softly uttered while he picked up his money, but his comment fell on deaf ears.

Grafton walked several streets over until he found the Fairfax Instrument Shop. It was nestled amongst several other venders in a red brick front five story building. The shop was full of modern calibrated instruments like telescopes, clocks, compasses, hourglasses and sextants. He wandered about the store for several minutes, examining the fare, before a sales person approached him.

The shop keeper noticed that he admired one of his rather expensive ship compasses. "That is a very nice piece, Sir, and we could give you an exclusive price."

"Yes it is rather a fine instrument." Grafton agreed. "However, what I really had in mind is a heliograph, but I don't see one here."

"My goodness!" he exclaimed. "We haven't sold one of those in several years, though I don't understand why. It is one of the best forms of communications over distance." He smiled, "you know the last time someone asked for one I sold three at once. Was that, by chance, you?"

"It was indeed, and I need another."

The clerk folded his arms and rubbed his chin in thought, then pointed his finger in the air. "Let me look at our books because we just might have one of those in our warehouse." Grafton continued to browse about the shop while the man searched for the item he needed. After several minutes he returned smiling ear to ear.

"One left." He mused with a satisfied smirk. "I'm afraid it is not the quality of the last three you purchased but it is portable and reflects from any direction. The best part is that I can sell it to you for only 75 dollars."

"Fine," Grafton answered, without pause at the price, and looked up from his study of the piece before him. "I will also take this sextant and that time piece over there." He pointed out a very expensive chronograph clock and brass sextant. "Have all these items delivered to my ship, the Bore Tide, at dock two, pier six on the waterfront."

"Yes, Sir, I will take care of that presently." He snapped his fingers for a junior clerk and explained to him about taking the items to the wharf. When he finished, he turned back to the Captain and thanked him for his business.

Grafton posted the money on his bill, then spent the rest of his leisurely afternoon strolling about the streets in the glorious summer sun. Even though it was a pleasant walk back to the wharf and the Bore Tide, the perils of his mission weighed heavily on his mind.

By the time Grafton got back to the dock, several wagons loaded with supplies had parked on the pier in front of his ship. The men busily slung boxes and crates by rope and pulley into the ship's forward hold. After coming aboard, Captain Grafton peered over the deck hold and observed the men painting over the ammunition boxes before they moved the cargo forward. "Very good, Mr. VanDorn," he shouted below.

The crewman looked up at his Captain and covered his eyes from the sun's glare. "Thank you, Sir, we should have everything loaded by night fall."

Grafton nodded and walked aft to where Mr. Cole stood and observed the men at their tasks. "There's a lot of equipment out on the dock, Sir, but it's going on nicely. We'll disassemble the wagons after they're," He stopped mid-sentence and looked over Grafton's shoulder down the pier. "Will you look at that!" he exclaimed.

Grafton turned and saw four sets of horses pulling cannon-type caissons, but instead of cannon, the two wheel carts hauled Gatling guns. "Damn!" Grafton whispered under his breath. "I thought they would be crated." He looked back and saw several men watching in amazement at the sight of the procession moving toward the ship. "What in the world are those things?" One of the men shouted aft to Mr. Cole but did not look back.

"Mr. Cole, get the men down there to dismantle those guns immediately. Wrap them up tight in canvas, then sling them aboard." As Cole turned to leave, Grafton grabbed him by the arm. "Tear down one caisson and we'll take it along, push the others over the side."

"Yes, Sir," he replied and hurried down the steps.

A carriage followed the procession of guns and it stopped next to the ship as well. Grafton watched an older gentleman, very well dressed in a stove pipe hat and white coat, get out and approach the ship. He came up the gang plank and walked directly to the lower quarter deck. He looked up at Grafton who stood near the rail at the top step watching him and shouted. "Are you the Captain?"

Grafton nodded and motioned for him to come closer. The man made his way up the steps, a bit out of breath from the climb, and reached his hand under the lapel of his coat. "Who are you, Sir, and what are you doing on my ship?" Grafton asked, but before the man could answer, Mr. Cole stepped up behind him and quietly placed a pistol barrel softly against his ribs.

"If I were you, I'd move that hand very, very slowly." Cole paused and whispered, "very slowly indeed."

The stranger turned his head toward Cole while his eyes drifted down to the pistol in his side. "My papers," he said and gently pulled them from an inside jacket pocket. He handed them to the Captain but kept his eyes fixed on the gun in his side.

Grafton opened the letters of introduction then folded them up to hand back. "It seems, Mr. Cole, we are to have a surgeon aboard this trip, courtesy of Mr. Stepp." With his eyes, Grafton motioned for Cole to remove the gun from the man's side. "Doctor Morrison is it?" He asked.

"That's right, Sir, Isaac Morrison, regimental surgeon with the Fifth Michigan, attached temporarily to this ship," he stated and removed his cap by the brim, tipping it to the Captain. "I must say I have had better receptions," he mused and placed his hat firmly back on, looking at Cole.

"Forgive us Doctor," Grafton shrugged, "for being overly cautious, but this is a Dutch ship in a foreign port and we are weary of strangers. Although we are a bit overcrowded in the officers' quarters, we will attempt to make your stay aboard as comfortable as possible. Have you ever been to sea, Doctor?"

"Never," he grumbled.

"Mr. Cole, have the Doctor's belongings moved in with Mr. Dobbs and I would be honored to have you dine with us tonight at 2000 hours."

"Thank you, Captain, I accept." he answered and Cole showed him back down the steps to his cabin. Grafton looked up and saw Major Bennett walking toward the ship with an agitated stride. When he reached the deck, Grafton asked him what was wrong. It turned out he could not locate his aide and the alcohol he'd consumed did not soften his disposition. Grafton came down the steps to confront the Major.

"You will contain your drink while aboard my ship, Sir!" He quietly yet sternly scowled at the officer. "If you endanger my men in any way because of it, I will personally toss you overboard." He looked directly into the astonished man's eyes, "Is that stark enough for you?"

Bennett nodded, clearly upset at the rebuke, but did not answer.

"Now," Grafton's mood mellowed, "what do you know of Lieutenant Overton's disappearance?" He asked.

"He was supposed to meet me here and it's very strange that he would not report back to our unit."

Grafton raised an eyebrow. "How much did he know about this mission, Major?

"The basic concept of the problem and that is all," Bennett snarled, yet lied. "Are you honestly suggesting he would betray me?"

"Yes," he paused. "I am." Grafton stated before he returned to the quarter deck. Bennett's shoulders slumped like a scolded school boy and he walked to his quarters.

Some more men returned from shore leave, so loading speed picked up with their assistance. It was nearly dark when they finally finished their tasks and the only thing left to do was lash it all down. Grafton told them to stand down for the day and ordered a portion of rum to go along with their evening meal. There was speculation about the use of the cargo brought aboard, but Grafton assured them they would be informed as, and when, the time came.

The evening meal for the officers was delicious and full of pleasant conversation. Major Bennett appeared to have completely sobered up from the afternoon affair and, it turned out, the Doctor was somewhat of a philosopher. He was a very knowledgeable individual on current events, a down to earth man with a likable personality. The hour was late when Grafton excused the men for an early morning. He had Mr. Cole stay behind in his cabin as the others left.

"If necessary, I want you to curry comb all the warehouses on the wharf tomorrow Bass," Grafton began. "We need to find as much sail cloth, spar timbers and bracing as we can take on."

"I take it you are expecting trouble ahead?"

Grafton motioned for him to take a seat. "We must trust no one on this mission if we are to succeed. The gold we seek is on a French Frigate and she carries 76 guns. If we can't bluff them out of it, we may have to fight for it."

"Do you really believe we can defeat a frigate?" he asked in astonishment.

"We can," Grafton paused. "And we will," he added with determination. "I have a few surprises in store should they put up a stink." He cleared his throat, "First things first, though. We will liberate Nelson Black in Richmond to help recover some papers I will need in Baja. While I see to that task, you will unload the Tide except for the cargo in the front hold and prepare to sail on a moment's notice." He smiled and shook his head at Cole's concern.

"If all of this works out and we don't get caught outright by the Confederate Army," he shrugged. "Then we'll worry about the French Frigate and I will inform the men of our task." Grafton stopped the briefing when a knock sounded on the door. "Enter," he shouted.

Dobbs stepped in and removed his cap. "Sorry to disturb you Captain but this man here just reported on board." He nodded his head to indicate the gentleman who stood behind him. It was Joseph Elder, his wagon master.

Elder looked exactly the way he should for his profession. He had long brown hair sticking out from under his western style hat and a large mustache. His gun belt was strapped over his open hip length deer hide jacket and pulled down above a pair of Union Army pants. His eyes revealed a mean look of a man one should stand aside for and a long scar ran across his right cheek and upper lip.

Grafton stood up, but did not offer his hand. "Welcome aboard, Mr. Elder," he said. "This is my first officer, Bass Cole, and, Mr. Dobbs, you've already met. I will see to some quarters for you with the officers so that you may keep your side arm. My crew is not allowed to carry weapons."

"That's fine with me cause ain't nobody gonna take my gun."

Grafton stepped past Dobbs and right in front of the westerner to look him directly in the eyes. "If you cross me, Sir, I will cut you into fish bait and feed your carcass to the sharks. You are under my command and will follow any orders I deem necessary to give."

A deadly silence ensued between the men for several seconds while they stared into each other's eyes. Elder sensed this man had the sand and tenacity to back up what he had just said and he instantly gained a measure of respect for Grafton. "Alright, Captain, I'll follow your orders," he growled.

Grafton did not shift his gaze from the man's eyes and said, "Mr. Dobbs see that this man gets quartered and have my steward find him a hot meal. We sail tomorrow afternoon."

Dobbs left with Elder and shut the Captain's door behind him. "That was interesting," Cole observed, "Any more surprise guests to come on board?"

"Just one," Grafton responded and looked blankly at the closed door.

CHAPTER V
IN THE HANDS OF GOD

It was a last day of peace before the aura of war would engulf them all. The crew of the Bore Tide knew little of what fortunes lay ahead or what perils the Captain had in store. Grafton slept in late and took his time about eating breakfast. His steward had brought in a morning paper with his food and Grafton took time to read at the table. After he cleaned and dressed, he made his way to the quarter deck where Mr. Dobbs was again on watch.

"Why isn't Mr. Cole on watch?" Grafton asked.

"Errand I believe Sir, he asked me to fill-in and then left the ship with several of the crew."

"Ah yes," Grafton remembered his request the night before. "Beautiful day, hey Mr. Dobbs," he smiled. "Let's hope Mr. Cole is successful on his errand."

"Sailing tide is 1900, Sir," Dobbs commented but did not look around. "If we are sailing today, that is?" He asked the question without really asking, trying to search for some indication of their schedule.

"We will see, Jeffrey, but that will depend on whether or not our last passenger shows up." Grafton looked around and up into the rigging where the mast flag fluttered in the breeze. "Looks like a fair wind if we do," he nodded. Joseph Elder walked aft from the main hold on deck and up the steps to where Grafton stood with his second officer.

"Been looking around Captain and we seem to have an awful lot of gunpowder and mass cases of special ammunition." He eyed the Captain. "It's only used for one kind of weapon you know."

Grafton and Dobbs exchanged glances. "That's right Mr. Elder, only one kind of weapon. If you must know there are four of them on board," he said while his attention was focused down on deck. "Mr. VanDorn." Grafton shouted and motioned for him to approach. "A word if you please."

VanDorn, dropped what he was doing and came aft to stand below the Quarter Deck and look up at the Captain. "Aye, Sir," he said as a question.

"VanDorn did you or did you not change the markings on all of those crates?" Grafton impatiently asked.

VanDorn looked down then back up before he answered. "Most of them, Sir" He shouted up, with one eye shut.

"I want them all painted over and remarked without exception. If Mr. Elder here can figure out our cargo, then so can the U.S. Navy," he admonished him.

"You expecting us to get boarded, Captain?" VanDorn asked with some concern.

"That is a risk we take every time we sail, Mr. VanDorn. Now get some help with those crates and see to your duty." Grafton's voice softened.

"Aye, Captain," he obediently replied.

"You are expecting trouble," Elder stated after the crewman walked away. "Perhaps that's why you wanted me along."

"Perhaps," Grafton replied and watched some crewmembers clean the deck.

He looked around at Elder who studied the rigging and rolled up sails with some concern.

"I ain't never been to sea before," he absent mindedly commented.

"Rest easy, Mr. Elder," Grafton smiled. "We have," he said and then returned to his quarters. Grafton spent the next several hours going over his new maps to check his plots from the night before. It never hurt to double check any calculations and estimates.

He was interrupted from his work by a knock on the door. "Enter."

Mr. Dobbs stepped into the cabin, "Beg your pardon, Sir, but I thought you would want to know. Bass made it back and is loading a bunch of sailing supplies and extra spar beams." He had a very concerned look on his face which did not go un-noticed by his Captain who leaned back in his chair and looked to the worried officer.

"Jeffrey, I intend to make every effort not to put the men or this ship in peril on our voyage. Unfortunately, I also believe that may not be entirely possible, but the rewards of this trip could be considerable. So I am willing to take the chance. In due time, I will explain everything to you and the crew."

"Yes, Sir," he nodded and turned to leave but stopped in his tracks.

"Oh, by the way, the men are all accounted for and on board. Also there are two prison guards in a paddy wagon with some man in shackles. They're on the wharf and asked to see you." Dobbs told him slightly confused about the situation.

Grafton smiled, "Have them bring that man here to me."

A few minutes later, Dobbs was back at his door with the three men. Both of the guards were in uniform and carried rifles. They gently pushed the old bent over man before Grafton's desk. "You have to sign for this one, Sir, before we can release him," the taller of the two guards said and pulled a paper out from his coat.

He outstretched the release paper over the desk. Grafton studied the old man before him who stared at the floor. "See to it, Mr. Dobbs." Grafton commanded.

Dobbs reached across the desk and grabbed the paper. He pulled a pencil from his tunic and scratched a signature on the bottom, then shoved it back at the guard.

"Take these shackles off him, if you please," Grafton waved his index finger across the man. "Then you may leave."

The guards did as requested in silence and left the cabin while Grafton continued to study his prisoner. The old man was shabbily dressed in prison garb and extremely dirty. He had been unshaven for a least a week and his long grey hair was matted down along the sides of his head. His eyes were sunken in his face and he looked somewhat undernourished. He finally looked up in the silence of the room at the Captain.

"Thank you, Sir, whoever you are, for getting me out of that horrible place." His voice was soft, but raspy.

Grafton got up and walked around his desk to look closer at the totality of the man who stood slightly slumped over and compliant. "What we have here, Mr. Dobbs," he started, "is a man by the name of Albert Reynolds Martrovich. He has a unique talent for masking legal documents and I believe is a relatively good forger. He is also a thief who just happened to get caught." Grafton looked at Dobbs. "The question is, however, is he willing to be a loyal citizen and do his duty to win this now ill begotten freedom?"

"I'll do anything you say, Sir, and follow your orders," Martrovich took a deep breath. "Just don't send me back to that hell hole."

"Good," Grafton smiled, "very good." He stepped up next to the beaten man and they made eye contact. "I have but one task for you, Sir, and when it is complete, I will set you free in the Confederacy or in South America or you may stay aboard this ship until we return to the Union." Grafton studied his face.

The old man smiled for the first time. "Your servant, Sir," he said and nodded.

Grafton nodded as well. "Mr. Dobbs," he said at last. "Mr. Martrovich smells quite foul and I do not want him dining at my table in these rags." He pinched a handful of cloth on the sleeve of his prison uniform. "Please see to it that he gets a bath and some decent clothing before supper."

"I'll be sure of it, Captain."

Grafton walked back behind his desk. "Also Jeffrey, tell Mr. Cole we will sail on the tide tonight so be sure everything is secured and no one leaves the ship from this point on. Tell the cook that I want the men to have a hearty meal before we depart."

Dobbs smiled broadly. "Yes, Sir. It is always good to get underway Captain, I seem to get kind of antsy when we just sit around." He put his hand on Martrovich's arm to guide him out of the cabin and the two men left.

The crew spent the rest of the afternoon securing everything for sea. Mr. Cole notified the Harbor Master they would depart and were in need of two harbor launches for tow out. At six the men were called to mess and Grafton dined with his officers, Major Bennett, the Doctor, Elder and Martrovich. Martrovich did not appear to be the same man Grafton had met earlier in the afternoon. He was now dressed in a grey wool suit with clean hair and had gotten a shave.

"A toast, Gentlemen," Grafton raised his glass of wine. "To a successful, and hopefully lucrative odyssey at sea, and may the wind favor the foolish."

The others raised their glasses as well, "hear, hear," they all exclaimed.

Everything was stowed now and the men were all on deck or up in the rigging. Grafton and the other officers stood on the quarter deck preparing to depart and watched the men in the harbor launches toss lines to the bow. "Captain," Cole shouted and pointed to the dock where a carriage approached at a quick pace. "We seem to have more company."

When he saw the coach, Grafton quickly made his way down the deck to the plank and over to the dock. The men tending the lines stopped what they were doing and watched him go to the door of the carriage to open it. "I am so glad you got my telegram and were able to make it here before we departed." He smiled, climbed into the rig and knocked on the ceiling for the driver to continue on.

"Just where does he think he's going?" Major Bennett asked with an indignant voice before he looked to Mr. Cole.

"He is the Captain, Sir, and he may go wherever he pleases." Cole snapped. "Mr. Dobbs belay our departure orders, if you please."

Dobbs shouted for the men on the deck and in the launch to stand fast until the Captain returned. It took about ten minutes for the carriage to come back, but then it sat in front of the ship for several more minutes before Grafton finally stepped out onto the pier. The men could see him still speaking with the unseen man inside before he closed the door and the carriage left. Grafton slowly walked back onboard, but stopped to watch the visitor disappear into the evening before he made his way back to the Quarter Deck.

"I demand to know who was in that carriage, Sir!" Bennett shouted.

"We have a stiff off shore breeze, Mr. Cole." Grafton commented while he looked up to the main mast flag.

"Sir," Bennett insisted, but when Grafton did not respond he added. "How do I know you didn't just jeopardize the entire mission with that clandestine meeting?"

Grafton turned around and snarled. "Because I'm in charge of this Goddamn mission, Sir, and you will not question my authority again or I will see you hanged!" Everyone on the deck heard the Captain impugn the officer and the small talk all but silenced.

Grafton angrily turned around, obviously irritated, and shouted over dockside. "Release the forward lines!" He stepped back across the deck and commanded the harbor boats to oar and the men in the forward mast rigging to set the top sail. Slowly the bow of the ship began to pull away from the pier and the last lineman scrambled aboard, pulling in the plank behind him. Grafton cupped his hand to his mouth and shouted. "Set the jib and staysail!"

The stiff wind caught the unfurling canvas and they briskly popped open. Grafton hurried back over to the dockside of the ship. "Release all aft lines!" In doing so the craft was now free of its moorings and moving forward. "Mr. Cole, cut those harbor launches free," he commanded before shouting, "Helm hard to port!" The helmsman spun the great wheel and the ship came about heading toward the outer inlet. When it did, Grafton ordered the rudder amidships.

He looked up into the rigging and shouted to set all mainsails and square away. His officers monitored all activities on the deck and directed the men as Grafton gave the orders to guide the ship out of the harbor. "South by Southeast is your course, Mr. Markell," Grafton quietly told the helmsman and looked back over his shoulder.

"Aye, Captain, South by Southeast it is." And he spun the wheel.

"Perfect night for sailing Captain," Cole said and smiled as he stood next to his boss.

Grafton looked up into the full sails and darkening sky, "Indeed it is, Mr. Cole. We should be in Richmond by day after tomorrow." He pulled his coat closer against the cool evening breeze. "When we are clear of the last buoy bring Major Bennett, Mr. Elder and Mr. Martrovich to my cabin. Mr. Dobbs will have the helm," he said before he retired to his cabin.

The men he requested sat gathered around the mess table while Grafton stood. "It is time I reveal some measure of our mission ahead and your involvement in it. The Major here knows most all of the details and the rest of you will be informed as the need arises."

"Just what is it we're after, Captain?" Elder asked.

"Cargo, Mr. Elder," Grafton responded. "A very lucrative cargo some distance from here. To secure it will require certain documents now locked in a safe in the basement of the First Presbyterian Church of Richmond."

"A church, Captain?" Cole inquired and turned to look up at his employer.

"Apparently the Confederates consider that location to be more secure than a bank," he shrugged. "In any case, we must retrieve those papers by stealth and deception replacing them with imposters." Grafton walked over behind Martrovich and placed a hand on his shoulder.

Mr. Martrovich here is a master at forgery and safe combinations. By coincidence, Sir, that is the job I have for you." He said and patted him on the shoulder.

"Exactly what are these papers?" Martrovich asked.

"It is more like a letter, I believe, from a high authority in the French government granting transfer of ownership to a certain cargo we intend to intercept.

"Oh," he cleared his throat. "Then the contents are irrelevant to forge as they can say anything. I seriously doubt anyone has read it in any case." Martrovich commented.

"Explain yourself, Sir." Grafton inquired curiously.

"Documents such as you describe come in pairs and are sealed only to be opened at the time of transfer by the parties involved." He shrugged, "You see, the two say the same thing, and at the appropriate time they are compared for authenticity after which any trading would take place."

"So what you're saying is that the holder of our cargo has a duplicate letter of that in the safe?" Grafton asked thinking about the possibilities.

"That's correct, Captain." He turned in his seat to look up at Grafton. "If another party, such as yourself, wanted to exchange one of the letters to use for other purposes, you could replace it with a blank sheet and the proper wax seal. No one would be the wiser until they attempted to exercise the document with the second party, at which time it would be too late." He tipped his head, "simple."

"Can you forge such a seal?" Elder asked him.

"If I have the time and proper wax," he said and turned his eyes to Elder across the table. "Yes, I believe I can."

"I will be sure you have anything you require, Mr. Martrovich, for the task at hand." Grafton patted him on the shoulder again. "Now for the rest of us," he began and paced in front of the others. "We are going to rescue a slave on the Langston plantation who will assist us in taking the church."

"A Negro slave," Elder said, almost under protest. "Why in the world would we need help from a common ignorant slave?"

"Nelson Black is hardly common, nor ignorant," Grafton smiled. "He is ten times more deadly with edged weapons than you are with that pistol. When we take the guards at the church we do not want to awaken the Army Post on which it sits with the noise of gunfire."

"How do you intend to get him out, Captain?" Cole asked.

"Jefferson Langston, who owned Nelson, was recently killed in battle so the old man who now holds him might be willing to sell. We will buy his way out of slavery if possible." Grafton looked at Elder. "If not, we will take him by force."

"That could complicate matters some, don't you think?" Elder quizzed him.

"It would certainly shorten the time we will have available in the church and hasten our departure from port," Grafton agreed. "Let us hope that won't be necessary. However, if it is, Mr. Martrovich, I want you to be prepared to work quickly. If worse comes to worse, we will just have to steal the papers and get out of there. Under no circumstances do we leave Richmond without the genuine article in hand."

"And what is my role here, Captain?" Cole inquired, "besides what we discussed earlier."

"As soon as we land, unload all the cargo bound for Richmond and prepare to sail. After you've unloaded, I want you to anchor off so we can make a hasty retreat. The four of us," Grafton pointed, "will rent a carriage and go directly to the Langston plantation to get Black. By the time we accomplish that it should be late on Saturday. We will then make our way to the church and see where we stand with the opposition."

Grafton took a deep breath and exhaled loudly. "By that time it will be very early Sunday morning. I shouldn't expect them to be very watchful, especially since there is no overt threat here in the capital. We will be obliged to take on the guards whatever their number." He looked at Elder and emphasized his last word, "quietly."

Mr. Martrovich will open the safe, forge the seal, and leave the false document. We will take any gold or money in the safe, mess the place up and make it look like a common robbery. The Confederates will find their precious paper and think the thieves did not know its value. Hopefully, they will think they still possess the genuine article and will not open it."

"You make the part about taking those guards sound simple,"

Bennett commented. "What if they put up a fuss?"

"Between Nelson, you and me, we'll just have to deal with it. I want one point clearly understood." He paused, "there will be no shooting unless your life is in danger." He looked around, "I believe there is the remote possibility that this place isn't guarded at all."

"Maybe we should find that out before we go rescue your Nigger." Elder suggested.

"It's immaterial, Mr. Elder." Grafton explained. "Nelson Black is a friend and I need him on this voyage. I intend to get him out of the South."

****

The Confederate Lieutenant stood up straighter so he could clearly see over the massive stone wall and picked up his eye glass to scan the darkening horizon. The white sails of the Bore Tide stood out against the black storm clouds far out to sea and glimmered in his glass.

The young officer turned to his subordinate sergeant and told him to roll out the cannons so they were prepared to fire. The sergeant protested that the Colonel had to be notified first. "Very well, Sergeant, go and find the Colonel but if you're not back by the time that ship gets in range I'll blow her out of the water."

Mr. Cole stood on the Quarter Deck with Captain Grafton and watched the fort through his eyepiece. "They haven't raised any flag yet, Captain."

"Very well, Mr. Cole, raise ours before they mistake us for Union and open up." Grafton replied. He reached over and took the glass to scan the fort for himself. "That's very odd," he said with concern. "Close reef, Mr. Cole, and slow us up some until we see their signal."

"Aye, Sir," he said and barked orders out of his cusped hands for the men to take in some of the sail.

Within short order the Sergeant returned with the fort's commanding officer who took a look for himself at the approaching ship. "What do you make of her?" He asked the junior officer.

"She just ran up a Dutch flag, but it could be a decoy, Sir."

The Colonel continued to look over the ship with a critical eye and he finally lowered his eye piece and snapped it shut. "Put up your guns, Lieutenant, that's the Bore Tide coming back from New York. Seems her Captain has been lucky again to evade the Union blockade. To my eye, she appears to be riding low in the water and I suspect he's loaded with Confederate supplies." He looked over at the nervous officer. "It would be a shame to sink her." He raised an eyebrow. "Stand easy Lieutenant," he smiled, "they're on our side."

The lookout in the crow's nest shouted down that the fort signaled a clear passage and Grafton belayed the reefing order. Major Bennett had changed into civilian clothes and now stood on the deck with the Captain. He looked up the mast, "What in the world is that contraption attached to the main spar, Captain?" he asked, while he cupped his right hand over his brow.

Grafton looked up as well, "It's a heliograph Major. Something your army should employ. The Romans and Greeks used those centuries ago to communicate over rather long distances. With the advent of Morse Code, I can now use them to communicate between my ships when we meet at sea." He looked back at the Major. "They are a useful tool and if everything goes as planned on this trip, we may have great need of them."

The Bore Tide eased its way up to a dock which jutted far out into the harbor from the edge of the trading community that had sprung up with the outbreak of war to supply Richmond. The Harbor Master held his papers on a clip board under his arm and stood on the wooden structure to watch while the men tied off the lines securing the vessel.

Mr. Dobbs got off the ship and informed the Master of their cargo so he could make arrangements for its transport. He also requested a carriage without driver for the Captain and some of his guests.

Dim light of the late afternoon settled in by the time the carriage arrived on Front Street. Grafton stood on deck along with the assembled men. "Mr. Elder, you will drive the coach and I want you," he looked at Martrovich. "You stay in the coach at all times. When we get to the plantation the Major and I will go to the house and attempt to negotiate with Mr. Langston." He shrugged, "From there we'll just have to play it by ear and everyone stay alert."

His steward came from the galley and handed Martrovich a covered bucket. "What's this?" Grafton asked.

"Hot coals for the gentleman, Sir." The crewman shrugged.

"Tools of the trade, Captain," Martrovich explained. "To warm the

Plaster of Paris and speed our retreat." He paused, "You did say that you might be in a hurry?"

The coach ride took the better part of an hour and Grafton rode on top with Elder so as to point out the way to the Langston plantation. It was dark when they pulled up in front of the main house but even in the low lights on the porch, it was obvious that it was a grand place. Grafton jumped down and the Major got out before the two walked up the path. Bennett opened the white picket fence gate and they made their way to the porch where Grafton knocked loudly on the door plate.

A black house servant dressed in a common calico dress with a white apron and red sash tied over her head answered the door. "Why if it ain't Misser Grafon, the old sea Captain hisself!" she laughingly said, in a jovial manner.

Grafton removed his hat and nodded, "Good evening, Martha, is your master, Mr. Langston in?" He shot a stern look to Bennett to remove his hat.

"Mercy no," she opened the door wider so they could step into the entry. "Young Misser Langston was killed you know and da Colonel took it real hard." She shook her head in pity. "The doctor came and made him move to town causin he's real worried bout da Colonel."

Grafton glanced at Bennett, "If the Colonel isn't here, Martha, who's in charge of things?" he asked.

"Oh, dat be mean ole Mr. Somerville, da overseer."

"And where might he be tonight?" Grafton kept up his questions.

Martha turned to look to see if anyone else was within ear shot and then looked to the floor, embarrassed. "He be sparkin one of da field hands down in hovel," she admitted.

"Where is Mr. Black?"

A real nervous look came over her face and she stuttered out an answer. "Misser Somerville took a bunch of white boys down there yeserday with guns and beat him before dey locked him up in da root cellar." Tears filled her eyes, "He says he's gonna hang Misser Black if Masser Langston dies."

****

Grafton pulled open the door to the root cellar and held up a lantern to make his way down the steps with Bennett and Elder in tow.

The yellow light cast an eerie shadow on the walls and barrels in the musty basement. Grafton spotted Nelson in the back chained to a ring in the wall. He set the lamp on a barrel and bent down to touch the unconscious man's shoulder.

The middle aged black man slowly opened his eyes, looked up and smiled. "Alexander, what an opportune moment for you to arrive. I was about to be invited to an uncomplimentary party in my honor."

"I came to get you out of here, my friend," Grafton informed him. "Are you able to stand and walk?"

"Of course. Their beating on me was to no avail, but as you can see they have me at a rather large disadvantage." He shook the heavy chain on his ankle.

Grafton nodded at Elder and pointed to the chain. Elder bent over with a hammer and punch in his hand, and in short order he was able to break the chain. All three men got to their feet and Black calmly dusted himself off.

"I need the help of your special talents Nelson and I'm afraid, my friend, it must be tonight." Grafton informed and asked him at the same time.

He looked at Grafton with affection in his eyes. "Mr. Langston elected to lock my weapons in a safe up at the main house and whether I help you or not, I shant leave here without them."

Neither Bennett nor Elder could quite comprehend that a black man could speak in such perfect prose and with an English accent or an educated tongue. It was also obvious to them that this particular black slave had an uncommonly large command presence about him.

They made their way back to the main house in the dark to find Martha waiting on the porch. She was there to keep an eye out for the overseer. When they arrived, she took them to the study and showed them the location of the hidden safe. It was a secretly located room stuffed in behind a bookshelf. Upon seeing it, Grafton told Bennett to get Martrovich out of the carriage and bring him to the house.

A short time after Bennett left, the double doors of the study crashed open and Martrovich stumbled across an area rug before he fell to the floor. Grafton and the others spun around to see the overseer, Somerville, holding a pistol to Bennett's back. One of his henchmen roughly pushed Bennett farther into the room. He looked at Grafton and slightly raised one eyebrow to suggest that he had been taken by surprise.

"Looks like we found ourselves a nice little party of Yankees to hang," Somerville growled. "You let that nigger loose to spy on the Confederacy and robbery of the Langston house," he shook his head and sneered. "Both are hanging offenses; and Martha," he looked at the trembling black woman. "I am amazed how easily you would betray your master after all he's done for you."

Elder turned slightly and shifted his weight to his right side. "Why don't you do yourself a favor and put that pistol away. If you do, I'll let you quietly walk out of here."

A cruel smile came over Somerville's face. "Not until I see this uppity nigger swing on a rope or die from my own hand. And when I'm done with him, you'll be next." He pointed the barrel of his pistol in the direction of Black to indicate who he was talking about. "What do you think about tha…"

He never got to finish his sentence. Grafton could not believe the speed at which Elder drew, cocked and fired his pistol. Before he could react to the movement, the bullet struck Somerville high in the right temple with blood, bone and brain matter splattering across the room. He dropped like a brick directly to the floor.

His accomplice had just started to move when Black swiftly pulled Grafton's dagger from his sash and effortlessly threw it some fifteen feet to hit the man in the throat which killed him instantly.

Martha grabbed her mouth to suppress a scream and quickly turned her head away. A wide grin formed on Black's face. "For many months I have waited for the proper moment to do that, Alexander." He looked around to Elder and nodded his gratitude. "I'm fortunate you brought with you the kind of man who acts rather than debates with tyranny."

Black went over to the dead man on the floor, knelt over and pulled Grafton's knife from his throat. "If you would be so kind as to retrieve my property from my late master's safe." He said and looked to a completely stunned Martrovich still sprawled out on the carpet, "We can get on with Alexander's business." He walked back to Grafton and handed him the knife after he wiped it off on his leg. "It would seem I have but little choice to help you now."

Martrovich easily opened the safe and Elder watched while Black retrieved his sword and dagger. It was the most beautifully engraved fighting weapon Elder had ever laid eyes on. Except for length, they were identical in form. While they were busy with that, Grafton took Martha out to the parlor away from the mess.

"Can you keep this quiet until morning?" He asked. "Perhaps just close off the study and not report the deaths until tomorrow."

"Yes'em," she answered. "It will be at least nine afore I find em there and it will take da boy a coupla hours to run to da sheriff. Da old cook is the only other person here an he won't say nothin."

They closed up the safe, turned out the lights and left the two men on the floor where they fell. After joining Grafton in the parlor, they all went to the coach and left the Langston Estate permanently. En route to the city center, Grafton explained his plan to Black, but until they arrived there was no way to know what odds they would face.

It was nearly one o'clock Sunday morning when they got to their destination. The only noise on the street was that of the horses from their own carriage. Elder parked some two blocks from the church and waited with the others while Grafton and Black went to have a look. Black returned in about ten minutes, telling them to follow him quietly.

The five men crouched in the bushes just down the street from the church and all was still quiet. "Nothing's moving and I haven't seen anyone about," Grafton whispered. "Maybe we're luckier than I thought." He looked back to the group. "Nelson and I will go have a look, the rest of you wait here until I signal."

They watched the two cross the short distance to the front door and go inside. There was just enough light outside to see only one door and it was at the very back of the entry parlor. Grafton slowly eased it open where he could see a stair and light shining at the bottom. He and Black made their way silently down with daggers drawn.

He peered around the wall at the bottom step into a well lit room. It was about thirty feet long and twelve feet wide. Mid way down, a guard leaned back in a chair sound asleep with his back to them. Grafton smiled and motioned for Black to have a look. He stepped up beside him. Upon seeing the sight, Black smiled and squeezed Grafton's shoulder.

He then threw his knife in the air to flip it and caught the blade. With his left hand on Grafton's shoulder he threw the knife with great force, but because it was launched blade back the butt end solidly struck the guard in the back of the head. He promptly fell out of his chair and hit the floor with a thud.

Black continued to smile, "No sense in killing some poor soldier at his post. Besides he'll be in enough trouble as it is come morning."

Grafton did not protest when he looked at Black. "I'll get the others," he whispered.

Once all the men were in the basement they had to work quickly. Elder stationed himself inside the front door of the church to keep watch. Martrovich came down the stairs with his bucket of now warm cinders and a black leather bag. There was a bank type safe on the far wall that took him about five minutes to open.

It appeared that several people worked in the basement during the day because the desks and several bookshelves overflowed with papers. They also found a locked door next to the safe which Bennett wanted to investigate, so he kicked it open.

Martrovich pulled open the massive steel door of the safe and it made a loud screech. On three of the shelves inside were several stacks of gold coins and what looked like a thousand dollars of Confederate script. The prize they sought was on a top shelf. "Here it is, Captain" Martrovich excitedly exclaimed.

"Well, get busy. Between your squeaks and Bennett's bangs the Confederate Army will be down on us any time," Grafton angrily whispered. He quickly glanced at the seal then went to see where Bennett had got off to.

Grafton found him in a small side room, next to a minting press ready for operation. Bennett slowly picked up a heavy steel rod on the floor and was about to smash it. "Leave that alone!" Grafton ordered.

"We destroy this and they'll be out of business for sure," he pointed at the machine in protest and then raised the bar to smash it. Before he could swing the club, the cold steel of Grafton's pistol touched his temple. Bennett stopped in the middle of his motions and cautiously glanced back without turning his head.

Grafton cocked his piece and the sound of the cylinder which rotated in Bennett's ear was deafening. "If you elect to swing that, I will splatter your brains all over the wall."

Bennett lowered the bar. "If you do, you could make me a Confederate hero. You really want to pass up a perfect opportunity to deny the enemy the very means to mint their coins." He angrily protested.

"For the last time, Major," he explained, "This is going to look like a common robbery and nothing more. You smash that press or destroy the stamp and they'll know we were here for other purposes." He motioned and waved his gun, "Now get out here." He stopped Bennett by the arm as he passed. "If we fail in this adventure, Major, I hope the South gets to mint their coin."

Martrovich worked quickly on the seal. He mixed and poured some plaster onto the seal and set it over the coals in the bucket. The wax melted but the plaster set up and he was then able to make a duplicate male seal from the remains of the first pour. He sorted through his can of waxes and selected the closest color match to make a new copy. The heated seal on the original was now broken and had to also be fixed.

"Captain," Martrovich whispered in his ear. "Do you want to read this letter before I seal it back up? This impression will not work very well more than once or twice."

Grafton picked up the letter and opened it but looked back at Martrovich. "Can you read French?" He asked.

"Of course," he reached out and took it from Grafton's hand and read it in silence. His eyes grew wider the farther he got down the page.

"Reseal it, Albert," Grafton warned in a low voice, "and keep the contents to yourself," he said and watched the old man's eyes light up.

Martrovich sealed it with his new plaster stamp and handed the freshly waxed letter to Grafton who put it in his coat pocket. "Pick this stuff up," he pointed at the wax, bag and bucket of coals. "Mess the papers up here like we ransacked the place and leave this." Grafton handed him the newly sealed false document, "in the safe where you found it." He smiled at the old man, "Help yourself to the gold coins and take some for Mr. Elder."

When they were finished they all met Elder at the top of the stairs. "Everything still quiet out there?" Grafton asked.

Elder looked back from his vigil through the open door crack. "So far so good," he responded. "There have been a few soldiers milling around now and again though."

Grafton looked concerned but they left the church anyway. As they approached the carriage, two armed soldiers looked over the rig. "Nelson," he turned and said quietly when they spied the two men. "Give Elder your weapons and keep your head down with your eyes to the ground." He motioned to Bennett and Martrovich to grab Black by the shoulders when they got closer to the carriage.

The pair spotted them approaching and leveled their weapons at Grafton. "Stop right there!" One of them commanded.

"Glad to see you boys on the job out here," Grafton responded and raised his hand with a smile. At the same time, he continued to walk closer to the men. "Just caught my nigger here," he nodded his head back towards the others who held Black. "We've been out most of the night looking for him after he jumped ship and stole my weapons. I'd turn him over to you here and now, gladly too." He lowered his hands as the two lowered their guard and he smiled a cruel smile. "Only problem with that is you'll just take him some where and put him to work," he paused and looked back. "I'm gonna take him back to my ship and hang him so the other blacks on my crew will learn they can't get away with theft."

"What's the name of your ship, Sir." One of them asked while he lowered the butt of his weapon to the ground to rest on the barrel. The other man tipped his musket down as well.

"The Dory Eagle," Grafton quickly lied. It was a ship he'd seen earlier at anchor in the harbor. "We sail tomorrow, so I'm glad we caught this one." He looked back at the others. "Throw his ass in there boys so I can get him back to the ship," Grafton motioned with his arm toward the door of the carriage. The two soldiers stepped aside and one even helped push him in. Black kept up his defeated stance, which completely deceived the two guards.

Grafton climbed up on the coach and looked back at the pair. "What's your name's so when I see your Colonel I can tell what a good job you two are doing."

"The younger one smiled, "Peters and Griffon, Sir."

"You boys take care now!" Grafton shouted down just before he slapped the reins to the horses and sped away. They made a hasty retreat back to the dock just as the light started to fill an angry dark clouded sky.

He pulled the carriage up short on the dock and told Elder to get Black and the others to the long boat. Grafton went into the Harbor Master's office to advise them he was about to leave port and keep him busy while the others left. The Assistant Harbor Master was curious why he didn't take on cargo for his trip back.

"Why are you going to leave empty, Captain?" he asked. "I mean, how will you be paid for all the goods you brought in if you don't take on cargo?"

"I have been in Richmond all night and made arrangements for just that," he explained. "My trading partners and I have reached an accord for other forms of payment." He walked over to the window and looked out to see if the others were now far enough down the pier not to be noticed. "I don't believe I owe you any more explanation than that," he said as a matter of fact with his back to the man.

"Of course not, Sir," he apologized. "I didn't mean to pry."

Grafton smiled, "If you would be so kind as to return the carriage outside with my compliments to the Harbor Master, I'll be on my way."

"I'll see to it, Sir."

Grafton was the last to climb aboard the Bore Tide from the launch and was greeted by the broad smile of Mr. Cole. "We are ready to sail on your word Captain."

"The word is given Mr. Cole. Get us out of here before they figure out tonight's events and hang us all." Grafton turned to Mr. Martrovich and a light sprinkle of rain started to stain his hat. "Forgive me for not setting you ashore," he smiled. "I fear you may not be welcome in this country after tonight."

"No apologies necessary, Captain," Martrovich tipped the brim of his hat. "I now know we are off to a far grander adventure which I would not miss for any reason."

CHAPTER VI
THE FIRST STEP

Mr. Cole directed the crew to get under way and oversaw weighing anchor. The sails filled with wind and snapped loudly when opened. They briskly shed the water pent up in the folds of cloth. A stiff morning breeze was on the prod and the Bore Tide responded to it well when she turned for a run down river to the open sea.

Some of the crew eyed the new colored man's arrival with suspicion and a feeling of uneasiness prevailed among the men, mostly because of concern over the recent actions of their captain. Grafton had noted this anxiety but let it pass for the moment, engrossed in his own problems.

"After we've cleared the Banks Mr. Cole, set a course south and away from the coast." Grafton looked to the angry sky. "We'll run with the wind while we can."

"Aye, Captain," Cole acknowledged and turned to look forward.

Grafton gestured for Black and Martrovich to accompany him to his cabin. When they arrived, his steward, Webster, came in and set a tray with cups and an urn of hot coffee on the Captain's table.

"I'll be back with your breakfast shortly, Captain," Webster said and bowed slightly in the captain's direction before he left.

"Mr. Webster," Grafton stopped him. "If you would be so kind to see to it that Mr. Black is taken forward to get cleaned up and have the doctor see to his bruises. Grafton turned and opened a chest next to the port side of his cabin. Inside was a folded set of white sail cloth clothing, a red silk sash and an Arabian turban headdress. He gently picked them up and handed them to Nelson. "With my compliments, Sir."

Nelson smiled a broad smile and displayed his straight white teeth. He raised the fabric to his nose to take in a long forgotten aroma. "Thank you, Alexander," he said with sincerity and shook the pile of cloth in his hands.

When they left his cabin, Grafton turned to Martrovich with a deadly serious stare. "What exactly did you read in that letter, Albert? I want it chapter and verse."

"Gold bullion, by God!" he excitedly stated, "more than fifteen million U.S. dollars worth of it to boot. All of it to be transferred at or near a town called Bahio Kino in Baja, California to a representative of the Confederacy. It is a gift from France to help upset Union exploits in Richmond."

"I believe it is meant to somehow help ensure the success of the Southern States in their secession. It would appear that France thinks to the future and a diplomatic liaison between their two nations." Albert cleared his throat and looked at the Captain, "Armed with this information, it doesn't take a mental giant to discern your destination or your purpose here."

"That's why I thought you might wish to come along and I didn't leave you in Richmond," he smiled. "Were there any stipulations as to the transfer?" he asked and tried to avoid the offhanded question of his purpose.

"Only that the bearer has the duplicate letter to trade to the ship's captain, which you now possess." He pointed toward Grafton's breast coat pocket.

"You will keep this information to yourself," Grafton said, as he poured two cups of coffee and smiled. "You did say the letter stipulated fifteen million?"

"Indeed it did, but there is something else, Captain." He shifted uncomfortably in his chair and picked up his coffee. "The parchment of the paper seemed less than royal and the seal was a little crude for that of other diplomatic documents I've seen."

"Are you suggesting we got a forgery ourselves?"

"Perhaps not, it may be the genuine article." he smiled, "Of course, you'll find that out when you meet the French. For you own safety, however, it is something you should keep clearly in mind."

****

Grafton was dressed, yet sound asleep, napping on top of his bunk to try and catch up on his long day's night. They had been at sea for several hours when Mr. Webster came in and shook him awake. "Captain," he said excitedly. "Mr. Cole says your presence on the deck is required immediately."

"All right," he sighed, and sat up on the edge of the bunk rubbing the sleep out of his eyes. "What is it this time?"

"A ship, Sir, it's off the port bow."

When the Captain came topside, Mr. Cole and Dobbs were on the quarterdeck next to Mr. Black and Elder. The wind bordered on a gale force and some infrequent large drops of rain stung their unprotected facial skin. Long strands of white water skimmed over the tops of the twelve foot seas in long streaks above the ocean surface. The ship carried all the sail she could muster for the conditions and pounded hard into the water.

"A ship!" Mr. Cole shouted to the Captain when he came up on deck.

Grafton cupped his hands to his mouth and shouted up to the crows nest, "Can you make her out?"

The crewman shouted back that it was a Union Steamer two points off the port bow and she was also carrying sail, catching up fast.

Grafton grabbed hold of a rope lashed next to the aft mast, to keep his balance on the pitching deck and looked down to the rain soaked wood to considered his options.

"I believe they mean to board us, Captain," Dobbs observed. He just got the words out of his mouth when the Union ship fired a shot over their bow.

Grafton tipped his head. "You may very well be right Mr. Dobbs." He spun around to look at his first officer. "Heave to, Mr. Cole, and lower our colors, we are about to have guests."

"But Captain!" Mr. Dobbs pleaded. "We must run!"

Grafton looked Dobbs in the eyes without emotion and shouted, "Heave to, Mr. Cole, and that's an order." He could see excitement in the officer's eyes about their approaching company. "Mr. Dobbs, go to the armory and break out the weapons, make sure every man is heavily armed."

Dobbs started to leave but Grafton grabbed a handful of his uniform sleeve and pulled him around close to his face. "You be sure they understand there will be no shooting on our part. This is a display of force only, because I want those Marines to know if they give us trouble it will cost them. We will talk, not fight our way out of this." He shook free of the man's sleeve. "No one shoots except on my direct order, do you understand?" He shouted.

Dobbs looked down at the hand which held him at bay. "Aye Captain," he said and looked back into Grafton's eyes.

The long boat had a difficult time in the crossing between the two ships but they finally managed to come over. Fifteen Marines and two officers boarded the Bore Tide in the late hours of their first day at sea. They were immediately surrounded by twenty five or so crewmembers, each armed with a pistol and repeating rifle. Mr. Dobbs pushed his way to the front of his men and tipped his hat to the boarding party's superior officer.

"What's the meaning of this?" The Naval officer demanded and waved his hand across the gathered armed men.

"Oh, I believe our meaning here is quite clear, Sir. Your men will remain on deck and you two officers will accompany me to the Captain."

The older officer angrily shook his head. "By God, Sir, you will have these men stand down and allow us to search this ship and its cargo or we will blow you out of the water under the legal authority of our blockade!"

"Then we can all die here" Dobbs pointed at the deck, "with you now if that is your wish," he insisted, "or you can take five minutes and discuss this matter with the Captain of the Bore Tide." He paused and looked at the outnumbered, wet and mostly frightened group of Marines. "Even though your company may have the resolve, Sir, a prudent commander usually talks before he commits his men to certain death!" he growled.

The officer could clearly see that his bluff was not going to work on the crew of this ship. With regret he asked to be taken to the Captain. "Stand fast men," he hollered back at his Marines before he accompanied Dobbs to the aft deck.

When they reached the top step the naval officer slipped, lost his footing and ran his knee into the wood of the deck. A hand appeared in front of him which he took and was quickly pulled to his feet. When his eyes lifted to his rescuer, his jaw dropped. Holding him firmly by the forearm was Nelson Black, the most intimidating man he'd ever laid eyes on. In the low light, he was almost an apparition of death itself in the form of a lord from an old Arabian book. The look on the senior seaman's face revealed he sensed there would be no quarter for him if his negotiations with the captain were to fail.

Nelson released his grip on the man and lifted his huge arm to point toward the rear stairs and the captain's quarters. His face showed no emotion whatever and his eyes flashed with disdain for the enemy now on the ship. The officer stumbled rearward, but kept an eye on the fearful sight of Nelson Black.

Mr. Cole pulled the cabin door open when Dobbs knocked and the three men entered. Captain Grafton stood behind his work desk which was covered with maps and charts. "My name is Grafton and I am the Captain of the Bore Tide. What is the meaning of firing on my ship, Sir?" he demanded.

"I am Lieutenant Commander Mathers, First Officer of the armed steamer, Boston, of the United States of America. We, Sir, are exercising our rights under blockade to stop and search this vessel for war contraband." He removed his hat and swatted water from the lower half of his coat.

"And we are sailing under a Dutch National flag on the high seas, Commander. I do not recognize your authority to be aboard my vessel." Grafton retorted.

"You have that right, of course, Captain, yet we hold the upper hand. If you wish to continue with this discord, we can arrange for your ship to go the bottom."

Grafton let out a long breath and dropped his pencil on the desk. "Mr. Cole, would you and Mr. Dobbs please give me a moment alone with these two gentlemen?" He asked. Both men nodded and stepped out through the cabin door closing it behind them. Grafton pulled open a drawer on his desk and handed a paper to Mathers without comment.

With a slightly confused look on his face, Mathers reached out to take the document and slowly opened it. His subordinate looked over his shoulder and also read. When he finished, he looked back at the other man and both had a look of disbelief. "How do I know this is not some elaborate hoax?" he finally asked of Grafton.

"I hope you noticed the signature at the bottom, Commander?"

"Yes, but that could be a forgery as well," he noted and slapped the top of the paper with the back of his hand.

"Perhaps," Grafton conceded. "However, it is not and I strongly suggest you accept it on face value because if you don't," he warned, "and you elect to disobey my orders, I will see both you and your captain hanged." He reached out and snatched the paper back. "This Presidential order makes me your commanding officer in this affair, Sir, especially aboard my ship."

With thoughts of the tense situation that lingered up on the deck and the larger than life Arabian guard at the door, it did seem prudent for the commander to accept the facts as presented. "Just what orders would you give?" he paused, "That is if I accept that letter as the gospel."

"You will remove yourselves from this ship and have your Captain stand down so we can be on our way without further interference." Grafton smartly replied.

"And if I don't?" Mathers pressed.

"Then we may very well go to the bottom, Commander, but I can give you my personal assurance that neither you, nor your men here aboard, will be afforded the discomfort of that event or, for that matter, will even know it's happened." He looked sternly at both men just before he smirked. "You have your orders gentlemen." Grafton walked around his desk to the mess table and picked up three glasses. He began to pour out some sherry while the two men stood in silence to ponder their situation. When finished, he picked up his glass and raised it in a toast.

"To the Honorable Captain of the Boston and her fine crew, a safe return from our mission and to the United States of America." Grafton stood still and held up his glass. The commander and his aide approached the table and took their glasses in turn, then drank the toast.

Mathers roughly set his glass down on the table and went to the door to leave. He stopped and looked back. "You know, of course, I will confirm this letter of yours," he raised an eyebrow. "Should it turn out to be false, the next time any American ship sees your colors you will be shot out of the water without quarter."

Grafton raised his glass toward the man. "I would expect no less from the U.S. Navy, Commander." The smile disappeared from Grafton's face, "Good day to you both, Sir."

Grafton took a moment to put on his foul weather coat before he went up on deck to watch the American Navy depart his ship. Some of the Marines had a devilish time getting back into the launch because of the heavy seas and Grafton's men made fun of them from the deck. When the launch was away and headed back to the Boston, he turned to Cole.

"Make sail, Mr. Cole, and get us out of here. I want to be well clear of any more blockade boats before midnight." He turned to look at Dobbs. "Disarm the men and lock everything back up. Also, make sure you have an accurate count of all weapons."

"Captain," Dobbs looked up at Grafton. "What did you say to make those men leave so easily?"

"What's the matter, Mr. Dobbs, you disappointed you didn't get to shoot anyone?" Grafton saw a broad smile on Black behind Dobbs at the remark.

"No, Sir." He shook his head with the knowledge he wasn't going to get an answer and he left to complete his task.

Grafton returned to his cabin and sat in the darkening room to watch the angry sea out of the aft windows. He slowly sipped a glass of rum and contemplated the dilemma of retrieving at least five million dollars more than his contract specified. It was certainly windfall information, but for who was the question that burned on his mind.

****

The next morning dawned with clear skies and a brisk northeasterly wind which made for perfect sailing. After he finished breakfast, Grafton made his way to the deck and took a few minutes to enjoy the morning air over the aft rail. Mr. Cole quietly walked up next to his captain and stood there with him in silence.

"All hands on deck, if you please, Mr. Cole," Grafton finally said in a loud whisper but did not look away from the shimmering sea.

Cole turned and walked forward to the deck master and gave the order to assemble the crew. Within a very short time all the men aboard were gathered just below the aft deck amidships. Major Bennett, Black and Elder, along with Mr. Dobbs, came up the stair to stand with Mr. Cole, who turned and informed the Captain that all were present.

Grafton came forward and stood before his crew. "Men, it is time you know what it is that lies before us. I have entered into a secret pact with the Union forces of the United States to recover some property they want from the French. As you may well have guessed by the cargo we took on in New York, this may prove to be a rather difficult and dangerous task."

He walked down two steps to get closer to the men. "We are bound to sail around the Horn," he paused when he saw the apprehension in his men's eyes about the dangerous crossing. "From there to Baja, California where we should encounter a French Frigate. My first intention is to take their cargo by stealth and cunning, but failing that, we will be obliged to take it on and seize their stores by force."

"Attack a frigate, Captain?" One man shouted and several of the men groaned in protest. "Are you crazy, Sir?"

"That's right Mr. Hitchcock," Grafton hastily replied. "Attack it, board it and seize the cargo. Remember, gentlemen, the crewmen of that French ship are mere sailors not military or combat veterans. It would be my guess they will not be prone to fight hard."

"Even though they out-gun us we will have the advantage and element of surprise," he looked around, "and before we arrive, you will all be well schooled for this fight and instructed in how to board a vessel at sea."

"It's all well and good that you made this arrangement, Captain, but it sounds like we're about to get ourselves killed." Johansen shouted from the crowd and shook his fist into the air as a protest. "What's in this for us besides adventure and your glory?"

"Fifty thousand U.S. dollars, to be divided equally amongst you." His remark silenced the group as they looked at each other in disbelief over the sum. Grafton raised his arm and held out his hand. "With luck we will not have to fight them at all."

"While in Richmond, we, that is, Mr. Black, Elder, Martrovich and I," he said and waved his arm backward to the men on the upper deck. "We managed to acquire a document from the Confederates which gives us the authority to transfer the French cargo. It is my plan to arrive in Baja ahead of some Confederate troops and to pose ourselves as that detachment sent to retrieve the goods. Then, with this document," he held up the paper, "we will trick them into turning their cargo over to us."

All the men now listened intently. "Make no mistake, men," Grafton assured them. "There are at least a hundred things that could go wrong and we may have to adapt our plans without notice. We may even get into the fight of our lives, for our lives." He emphasized.

"However, great rewards require great risk, but only for those who are willing to take it," he shouted and shook the paper in his raised fist.

He stopped while his gaze wandered over the quiet men on the deck. "Over the next few days," he started again and with a lower voice. "I want you all to consider these risks and decide for yourselves if it is worth the reward and whether you are in or out of this scheme."

"Let me assure you that any man who does not want to get involved will be put ashore at our next stop, Rio de Janeiro, and with no hard feelings. If I am still alive upon conclusion of this undertaking, I also assure you that I will return to pick you up or, if you wish, you are free to sign on to another ship in port.

Quintin looked up at the Captain from the lower deck. "What's so important about this cargo, Captain, I mean what kind of stores do they want us to pick up?"

"A valuable cargo, Mr. Quintin," Grafton gazed up to the sky and tried to decide if he wanted to tell the men about the gold. Finally, he elected to wait and looked back at the men before he spoke. "It's the kind of cargo which will put a lot of money in your pockets should we succeed."

Hearing no more immediate questions, Grafton changed the subject. "I estimate no more than twenty four days to Rio if this wind holds. We will pick up ships stores for the journey about the Horn through the Drake Passage." He looked down, then back up, "Although it has its challenges, it is by far the safer and faster course to the Pacific." He smiled. "We should be able to be around the continent by late August."

One of the men shouted that the Horn was most likely more dangerous than the Frogs and everyone nervously laughed.

"I have been around the Horn three times men, but only once in a strong gale." He paused. "This is a good time of year, but should we run into weather, it will be a story you can tell your grandchildren when they ask of your adventures with the sea. The Tide is a sound ship," he tapped his palm on the hand rail, "as you know, and it can weather any storm as long as we keep our heads about us."

Grafton nodded in approval at the resolve of his men. "Return to your duties now men and think over our talk here this morning." He turned and went back up the steps to the aft deck. He did not turn or look back, but quietly asked Mr. Cole if the men were dispersing to their stations.

"Yes, Sir," Cole smiled, "I think you have won them over."

CHAPTER VII
RIO DE JANEIRO
AND THE SEA

"Land Ho!" Came the call from the crow's nest twenty three days nine hours after the crew had met with the Captain on deck. "Dead off the bow, Captain!"

Grafton pulled the pocket watch from his jacket and compared it to the ship's clock just above the chart table on the aft deck next to the boatswain's wheel. He snapped it shut with a smile and looked up at Mr. Cole who also studied the map. "Right on the hour and right on course."

"Very good Captain," Cole responded, "It is always a pleasure when one's calculations are confirmed."

"Indeed." He tapped on the map with his index finger. "Turn south in one hour, then run for two more hours on a tack course and we should be abeam of Rio." Grafton looked up to the crows nest and the flag atop the main mast. He could see the wind was with them on their course. "We shall spend as little time as possible in port, Bass. Get the stores we need along with as much fresh fruit as you can find. I don't want the men to leave the ship unnecessarily now that they have agreed to see this journey through."

Major Bennett came up on deck and walked up to the Captain. He asked if he had heard correctly that land had been sighted.

"Yes," Cole smiled. "It would seem it has not been misplaced after all and we found it right where it was supposed to be."

"Major Bennett," Grafton looked up from his map. "After we sail from Rio, I will have our carpenter, Mr. Vanderhaas, build mounts for three Gatling guns. One aft, one amidships," he pointed, "and the other one on the bow." He leaned back against the table and folded his arms. "You will instruct several of the men in its operation and pick out those who show the most promise of accurate marksmanship. Under no circumstance will we expend more than 15,000 rounds on each gun in practice."

"That should be a sufficient amount for training, I should think," the Major nodded.

"You will also assist Mr. Elder who will instruct them in the use of the repeating rifles and pistols until they are proficient. All of the men will be needed for a boarding party should that become necessary, so be certain they can all shoot well." Grafton turned and dropped his pencil down on the map table.

"Mr. Black and I will help them in the use of the sword and some basic tactics for self defense." He drew a deep breath. "We will persist with this training for the rest of the voyage, Major. Not only will it give them confidence in our task, but it will take their minds off the dangers at hand and keep them busy."

The Major raised an eyebrow and tilted his head. "What shall we shoot at for practice out on the high seas?"

"We will rig a target raft and tow it behind the ship." Grafton nodded his head to the stern. "They can take turns shooting at it from there."

****

The hour was late when they sighted the lights of Rio, so Grafton decided they would stand off shore until morning to make port. He did not want to risk damage to his ship in the dark and his decision to await land was correct. The early hours of Aug 4th revealed clear skies and brisk offshore southeasterly wind, which made docking tricky.

After three tries they were finally secure to the wooden jetty. Mr. Cole readied a party to secure the supplies they needed for the last leg to Baja. He led it himself and by late afternoon supplies began to arrive on the dock carried on the backs of native slaves.

The rest of the crew remained busy loading the stores from the long procession of human workers that filed down the pier with their heavy loads. Nelson Black watched from amidships, disgusted at the way his countrymen were being prodded by the overseers.

A short, slight built, black girl stumbled on the dock near the bow of the ship. The wood splintered around her knee and she dropped her large bag of rice which broke open and the white contents danced over the slippery boards ahead of her. Black watched her scramble forward and begin to shovel the grains back into the bag, but to little avail. A large white man in a floppy fedora stepped up behind her and began to swat her back with a cat'o'nine tails. This indignation was more than Black could tolerate.

He tied a load pulley rope to the rail, then grabbed the other end to swing over the deck. His bare feet hit the wood pier with a snapping sound and in a wink of an eye he made the five or so steps to the frightened girl. Her tormentor raised his hand to strike her for the fifth time, but Black's sword cut the weapon off at the nub in one blindingly fast swing. Mr. Elder had watched him slide over the rail and now observed the events unfold from the ship's deck as well.

The surprised overseer looked in amazement at the end of his destroyed enforcer's weapon before he threw it to the dock. "No darkie is going to do something like this to me and live to brag about it," he screamed in Portuguese. Though he didn't recognize the language, his meaning was clear to Black, especially when the man pulled a revolver from the front of his wide black belt and cocked it.

At the same instant Black could hear the sounds of footsteps from two other people running up behind him. His sword flashed again toward the overseer, only this time three fingers from the man's right hand were sliced off. Blood followed the blade's arc until it impaled itself in the stomach of a second overseer who had come up behind him. Both men fell to the dock and screamed in pain. For one, it would be his last.

Black spun around in time to see the third man run toward him, with his arm in mid air. He tried to swing his whip into the swordsman's face, but Black's blade sliced through the extended arm, severing it from his body. The instigator of the entire affair struggled to pick up his pistol with a shaky left hand and shoot Black. He managed to raise the gun to do the deed, but Black shoved his sword through his neck and out the spine, killing him instantly.

He put his bare foot against the man's chest and pushed him over backwards withdrawing the blood stained blade. In doing so he glanced up to see another large bearded man about fifty feet down the pier. The man raised a musket and leveled it in his direction. Black swallowed hard, thinking it was likely over for him. He was about to jump sideways when the crack of a weapon reached his ears. That sound, however, came from Elder's pistol, up and behind him on deck of the ship.

Suddenly blood poured over the man's face and the musket slipped from his hands, falling to the wooden dock with a thud. He also fell straight down to his knees, with a hole just over his left eye, before he dropped face first to the boards. Black looked back to see Elder spin the pistol by the trigger guard and rotate it neatly back into his holster with a smile of satisfaction. It was an incredibly accurate shot for the distance.

Grafton heard the shot and came up on deck to stand next to Elder. Several people pointed from shore and shouted about the commotion on the pier. They were clearly upset that their countrymen were being accosted by the strangers. He looked down to the carnage on the dock and knew it wouldn't take long for the angry spectators to grow into a mob. Grafton also watched as Black grabbed the female by the arm and pulled her to her feet.

She fainted into his arms from the heat, the whipping and the sight of the dead bloody men lying around her. Black slid her body over his shoulder and climbed the side of the ship, using the load rope to get up to the deck. Elder waited above and held out his hand to pull them both over the rail.

Grafton turned to the stern and shouted back to his second officer, "Mr. Dobbs, fire three blank cannon shots to seaward." He looked at Elder, "Hopefully it will alert Mr. Cole that we have some trouble." He glanced back to the pier. "You men there," he pointed, "swing that last load aboard and climb up." Grafton turned again and shouted louder, "All hands on deck!"

The men scrambled topside, somewhat confused by all the activity, but Grafton was clearly in charge. "Cast off all lines," he commanded from the mid deck, "Set the topsail and spinnaker and bring us about." He grabbed a crewman's arm as he ran past. "Set out a launch with three men to await Mr. Cole at the pier."

"Yes, Sir, Captain," the man acknowledged.

Elder stepped up next to Grafton and looked over the side. "I'll accompany those men if you don't mind?" he asked.

Black gently laid the female on a pile of ropes near the hold and looked up at Grafton. "Mr. Elder and I will both see to the safe return of your first officer and men, Alexander." He exchanged glances with the westerner. "For it was I, after all, who started this tippet."

"Very well," Grafton agreed. "We will lay off just far enough so it would be difficult to be boarded by a mob." Just then three shots erupted from the starboard side cannon and echoed across the bay.

"That should bring Mr. Cole a running." Grafton smiled and returned to his duties on the aft deck.

The men pushed the launch over the side and lowered it to the water as the front of the ship slowly arced away from the pier. Several men scrambled over the side along with Elder and Black. Grafton continued to maneuver the ship downwind and away until they came some one-hundred yards from the end of the pier. It was there he ordered the anchor lowered and the sails reefed. He spent the next several minutes watching the city wharf through his telescope and searched for his men among the crowd.

When Elder and Black re-appeared on the pier, most of the people who were left there began to quickly move off. They did not want any more problems from these two most dangerous men. However, the crowd on shore became much more hostile and their chants more intimidating. Cole and several men appeared on the street just above the mass of people and tried to make their way through the mob. Suddenly a lot of pushing and shoving started between the two groups.

Another loud cannon burst thundered over the bay from the Bore Tide, only this time the roar of a large iron shot screeched over their heads and burst into an empty shed some distance from the commotion. A loud moan came up from the people on the street and many of them ran for cover. This was just the opportunity Cole and his men needed to make it safely back to the pier. Their two rescuers, Black and Elder, ran up to meet them half way and stood between Cole's men and the mob with swords and guns drawn until everyone was in the boat.

When they at last departed the pier some members of the crowd ran out and began to throw rocks at the men, but they were out of range. The stone projectiles splashed into the water; clearly their attempted assault was in vain. The men in the launch put their backs into their oaring as if they had to row for their lives.

"What started this mayhem?" Cole demanded and wiped his brow.

"I'm afraid that I did." Black answered. "It didn't seem quite proper to allow a brute of a man to pummel a slight girl with a whip, what. Unfortunately, his friends protested my interference and it became necessary to dispatch some of them."

As soon as the launch reached the side of the Bore Tide, ropes were lowered to attach it to the ship for a lift. All of the men climbed over the side, glad to be out of harm's way. "Good to have you aboard, Mr. Cole," Grafton smiled, seeing his first officer climb the steps to the aft deck.

"Captain," crewman Hobson shouted from the lower deck. "It looks like we got well over half of the stores loaded before we had to shove off."

"Very good man," he replied. "See that everything is secured below now." Grafton looked to Mr. Black who tended to the female on deck. "Take her below and get Doctor Morrison to have a look at her, Nelson," he ordered before he returned to the duties to get his ship back at sea.

****

Nelson gently laid the unconscious girl on a make shift bare wood table which had been set up in the doctor's quarters for any future needs he might have of it. He lovingly brushed the hair away that was stuck to her face. Doctor Morrison came up behind him and handed him a lantern to hold over the girl's body. He confirmed her heart and breathing were normal and started to check her over for any broken bones. Morrison walked around the table and could see the concern on Nelson's face for the waif.

"Nothing serious, I should think," he commented. "Just stress, the heat and possibly poor nutrition over the past months." He shifted his body and tilted his head to examine her neck and jaw. "Help me turn her over and we'll see to the lacerations on her back."

The two men turned her over and the doctor pulled apart the torn cloth on the back of her Calico dress. He ripped it open to her waist. There were several wide red marks and some patches of wet blood. Morrison turned and poured some water from a pitcher into a bowl before adding iodine to the mix. When he touched her wounds with the cool cloth, it stung and caused the girl to moan and partially wake.

"Easy girl," Nelson's deep baritone voice quietly reassured her along with the soft touch of his massive hand on her cheek. "You are safe aboard the Dutch vessel, Bore Tide, and the good Doctor here is seeing to your wounds." He bent over and looked into her coal black eyes. "You're among friends," he smiled. She reached out and took hold of his forearm to squeeze it but did not speak before closing her eyes.

The Doctor completed his work and, with Nelson's help, assisted her to sit up on the table. She quickly grabbed the front of her dress with both hands to keep from exposing her breasts. "She'll need some new clothing I'm afraid, and the only things available are shirts and pants."

"Then that will have to do." She softly spoke in English as she turned to look over her shoulder at the Doctor.

"You speak English then," he smiled. "That's fine."

"I learned several languages when I worked at the house of Carlton on the Green Briar Plantation, English was one of them."

"If you were a house slave, why were you on the dock today carrying bags of rice?" Nelson asked, somewhat puzzled.

"My madre, I mean my mother, died last month. The overseer took me for his desires, but when I refused to please him he put me to field work. My master didn't object either because he wanted me out of the house before his young son started to use me." She drew a deep breath, "It doesn't matter anymore."

"What's your name, girl?" Nelson asked.

"Rita," she sadly smiled. "No one has asked me that question in a very long time. Rita Perez."

The Doctor bowed his head slightly. "I am Doctor Morrison and this rather impressive gentleman is Nelson Black." He stepped over to the door and pulled it open. "I will endeavor to find this young lady some clothes." He said before he left the two alone in his state room.

"Thank you, Mr. Black, for saving me from that awful man." She reached out and touched his arm. "My life is in your debt."

Nelson looked down at the lovely supple fingers caressing his arm and the usual harsh look in his eyes softened. When he glanced back to her eyes, her loving stare naturally stirred his basic instincts. "You owe me nothing, Miss," he reassured her. "Until recently I also was a slave but in the Confederacy."

"I find it hard to believe you would have made a good slave, Sir." She smiled and looked down from his gaze to conceal her own desires.

There was a knock on the door just before it burst open. Captain Grafton stepped inside and looked angrily at Nelson. "Our Doctor tells me you can speak English, Miss," he stated and turned in her direction.

"Just what am I supposed to do with you now that Mr. Black here has made you our guest?" His hostile attitude somewhat subsided when she smiled and he took his first good look at the young black girl. She was in her late teens with extremely fine features and an olive complexion. Her long black hair was straight and silky, indicating some Spanish or Inca blood lines and her smile was infectious with perfectly aligned white teeth. Grafton cleared his throat, slightly embarrassed.

"You were saying, Alexander," Nelson smiled at his distress.

"Well, yes," he stuttered and turned his gaze back to Nelson. "We'll find a spot for her to be useful on this trip." He put his hands behind his back before he walked toward the door muttering. "It will have to be somewhere away from the crew, I should think."

"I am a very good cook, Sir," she quickly interjected before he stepped out.

"Huh," he observed, and shook his head. "My steward will love to hear that!" Grafton nodded his good byes and left, stepping past the Doctor who returned with some clothing.

"Here you are, Miss," he pushed out an arm full of sailor's garb. "It's all I could find," he apologized.

"It will do just fine, thank you Doctor," she smiled.

The two men stepped out of the room while the girl changed into the new clothes. She winced while putting on the shirt because the cloth stung her when it touched the wounds on her back. Except for these new marks, her long sleek body was smooth, supple and without flaw. When she finished with the new wardrobe she pulled her long hair back into a pony tail and tied it off with a ribbon.

Nelson waited outside the door when she came out. "I'll take you to the Captain's steward and we'll find you something to eat." He held out his arm for her to walk past and up the steps to the deck.

Several of the men attended their duties when the two came topside and it was obvious they were none too happy to have a woman on board ship. Her presence was even more disconcerting to them with the very dangerous Horn of South America ahead and a female in their midst could only mean bad luck.

****

Eight days had passed since they left Rio under less than desirable circumstances and now it was the doldrums for the Bore Tide. Sailing winds had been poor but now they were adrift on a calm ocean and the glassy water had not abated for two days. The sails hung un-fluttering, like giant white cotton blossoms on their branches against the absolutely clear blue skies. Not a breath of wind could be felt on the air and the heat, along with the intense humidity, was nearly unbearable. To make matters worse, target practice had not been going well, which made the crew feel as if they might be doomed against the frigate and their stress began to show.

Grafton stood over his chart table on the aft deck to take a sextant shot on the setting sun. He completed the shot, made his calculations and looked over at Cole. Grafton wiped the sweat from his brow with two fingers and snapped the moisture off to the deck. "It looks like we are drifting northeast on a four knot current," he commented with slight disgust. "At this rate, we will be back abeam Rio in two weeks."

Cole looked to the sky, "Maybe the weather will change tomorrow, Captain," but after some reflection he added, "No, I don't believe it will."

Grafton dropped his pencil to the table and leaned back against its side. He stood in silence for a moment and listened to the sounds of the ship's creaks and of the coming night. "The men are very quiet this evening," he commented, lost among his thoughts, almost as an after thought. "Do you suppose everything is alright?" he asked.

The main mess was seething hot with a stove that burned in the corner behind the serving table. Most of the men were soaked in their own sweat. Rita Perez stood next to the steward to dish out stew in the bowls of crewmen who waited in a long line.

"You're in my seat, Quintin." Hitchcock growled at the crewman seated on the outside corner of one of the long tables after he got his bowl filled.

Quintin looked up at the man who held his bowl of stew and bread. "Bugger off mate," he grumbled in reply, before he looked down at his own bowl.

Hitchcock threw the hot soup over Quintin's shoulder and chest which brought an immediate response. He was on his feet in a flash, but Hitchcock dropped him back over the chair with a sharp right jab to the jaw. After the strike, he jumped him and the two began to roll on the floor, gouging at each others faces. The other men in the mess cleared back to give them room.

Quintin surely got the worst of the beating from the younger man. Hitchcock had clearly won the fight but refused to stop the assault and let his rage get the better of him. Suddenly he was plucked up from behind and thrown over the mess table to the floor on the other side. Still in a rage, he scrambled to his feet.

"I should think that would be quite enough." Nelson Black stood before him with his hands on his hips. "You've made your seating arrangements clear and this man doesn't need to suffer any more of your wrath."

Hitchcock fumed with rage, hatred and stress, which reflected and welled up from the entire crew over the past several days. He pulled a knife out from his belt and menacingly pointed it toward Black. "You don't need to meddle in this and I am not afraid of you or any other darkies!" he shouted. "I could carve you into little pieces now that you're without Grafton or Elder to back you up." Although he had made the threat and there was no way out of it, fear in his eyes told Black that he was clearly a man in a desperate corner.

Black slowly pulled both the sword and dagger from his sash and calmly laid them on the table before Hitchcock. "You must do what you think best, Samuel, but if I were you, I'd keep that knife," he pointed. "You're going to have need of it."

Hitchcock lunged across the table at Black, swinging the knife violently toward his chest but to no avail. Black simply side stepped his movement and easily removed the knife from his hand as he passed. Hitchcock found himself spread flat out, belly down, on the floor near Black's feet.

He quickly jumped up and spun around, somewhat disoriented. Black flipped the knife in the air to catch it by the blade. "You attack out of anger and off balance, Sir, and you are not rational." He held out the knife for him to take it back. "I believe this is yours?" Black mocked him.

Slowly, Hitchcock took the knife back by the handle and looked at it, then up into Nelson's eyes. He lunged again without warning, only this time tried to stab directly into his midsection. Again the knife was swiftly removed from his hand and Black spun him around, pulling him into a neck hold. He placed the knife against his jugular. "A child could defeat you in your rage, Hitchcock," he whispered into his ear.

Black pushed him away but not hard enough for him to fall. Hitchcock quickly turned around and Black threw the knife where it stuck in the wood floor at his feet. The room was completely silent except for Vanderhaas, who helped Quintin to his feet. "You men are doomed to lose this upcoming battle with the French." His remark was directed at Hitchcock, but for the benefit of the entire room.

"We're just simple sailors," VanDorn observed, while he continued to help Vanderhaas pull the beaten and bloodied man to his feet.

"You are men like any others!" Black shouted in rage with a clenched right fist and shook his arm in the air before he lowered his voice. He looked over the silent room of sweating and frightened men. "Sailors, carpenters, scribes, blacksmiths or warriors can not overcome adversity until they first overcome themselves. If you do not believe you are worthy, you can not win."

"Can you teach us how to be worthy?" someone asked from the back.

"Ah yes, that's the question isn't it." He nodded and looked around with a half grin on his face. "But the real question should be, can you listen and are you ready to learn?"

Some of the men answered yes, while others stood in silence. Black looked to Hitchcock when he asked the question, knowing he was one of the informal leaders among the crew. He bent over to briskly pull the knife from the floor and hand it hilt first to Hitchcock. With both men holding on to opposite ends of the knife, he asked again, only this time looked directly into his eyes. "Are you ready?"

The two men continued to stare at each other and at long last Hitchcock answered. "Yes." A sigh of relief passed over the room and it seemed as if some of the recent collective stress vanished.

"Good," Black smiled, "We will start in the morning," he said and released his hold on the knife. He turned, picked up his weapons from the table and stepped out of the mess. Grafton leaned against the wall in the dark, next to the door out side of the cabin. He had stood there and listened to the altercation among his crew.

"You handled that rather well, I thought," he said and let out a breath.

Black smiled and placed a hand on Grafton's shoulder. "They are good men, Alexander." He squeezed him and walked away without further comment.

The morning sun brought no relief or pity from the relentless heat. The silence of the sea was so un-nerving that it stirred fear in a man's heart and played games with his mind. An eerie atmosphere held the ship in its grip and surrounded it like the glass of a bottle. Not even a whisper from the planet itself could be heard this morning on the wood deck, but Black had the men line up in rows anyway and ignored the seemingly bad omens.

"I want you all to drop down to your knees and sit back on your heels." He commanded while he walked up and down the four rows of men. Some grumbled but they all did as he asked. "Close you eyes and clear you minds. I want you to all breathe slowly and deeply and try your best to relax." He kept walking along the rows and spoke in a soft voice.

"Feel no anger toward anything or anyone. Try to find peace in the quiet reaches of your minds. Be at one with this world and all its powers, feel Providence and accept what you can not change." He stopped and sat himself before the men. Grafton, with his arms behind his back, along with the doctor and Bennett, stood on the aft deck to watch. Now, not only was the ocean silent, except for some of the wood bracing, so was the ship.

After a few minutes Black stood and aroused the men. One joked that he had nearly fallen asleep. "That's excellent," Black replied. "It means you were relaxed. You must practice this anytime you can spare a few minutes, and we will try to do it every morning from now on."

"What does this have to do with beating those damn frogs?" A cry came from the back.

"Remember," he paused, "First you must conquer yourself before you can succeed." Black cautioned. "Inner peace is vital and the ability to remain calm even when surrounded by adversity is paramount. You are not angry at nor do you hate the French. We simply want to defeat them and take their cargo with mercy, compassion and without hatred."

Black paused and put his arms behind his back. "Last night, when I disarmed Hitchcock, it was simple for me to do because he could not think in his rage. With a few basic moves, you too will be able to conquer the Frenchmen in a similar manner. When we board the ship their officers will be irate, or already dead, and the crew will be disoriented and scared. Both are states of mind which will cloud their ability to fight. You men, through this mental exercise and practice, will not be so encumbered."

The rest of the morning Black spent on instruction in hand to hand combat. He demonstrated how to disarm and attack a man from his weak side by either removing the weapon or the ability for him to use it. Elder and Bennett took some of the men aft to practice their rifle skills and gunshots were the only noise in any direction. At about eleven, Grafton summoned the crew amidships, which brought an end to the training.

He stood at the front of the aft deck and looked down at his crew, "It appears that we may be stuck here if the wind doesn't return." He cleared his throat. "There is a good chance at this latitude that it won't for some time. Therefore, we are going to pull our way out of this doldrums with the longboats." He looked down and paused. "I am not pretending this will be easy and I estimate that we will have to cover 90 to 120 nautical miles."

"We will put out three boats and work in two four hour shifts each. And everyone, including myself, will stand a watch. My calculations show that we are drifting north on an ocean current, so I have instructed Mr. Cole to rig a sea anchor to help hold our position when we are not rowing." Grafton looked over a very sullen crew. "As soon as Mr. Webster prepares a hearty meal we will start out on this endeavor." He turned away but stopped and looked back at the quiet group. "Rest now men, we will all need our strength." He nodded. "Dismissed."

"This course of action did not seem to set well with the men, Captain." Mr. Cole commented in his ear after the men began to break up on the mid ship decks.

Grafton turned to watch the men wander toward the forward mess cabin and scowled. "The hard work will keep their minds occupied and their bodies tired." He turned his head to look at Cole. "Let's keep our female guest to the aft cabins for the time being."

Cole seemed puzzled at the request but only nodded in understanding of the command. She had been acting assistant to the steward to do some baking and serve food to the men.

"She may be bad luck as far as the crew is concerned," Grafton finally added, "But as time passes their basic desires will prevail and there may well be problems."

****

Grafton was the last man on the left row in the launch. He pulled hard on one of the oars and had a cloth tied around his head to keep the sweat out of his eyes. His hands were wrapped in sailcloth rags to protect them against blisters. The Bore Tide loomed like a giant beast about twenty yards behind them as it rose and fell on the quiet sea. To his left and right the other two boats full of men labored on their task to move the large craft, and the only disturbance in the water was the white bubbles which swirled off in unison from all the swinging oars.

Sweat still managed to reach Grafton's eyes and parched lips. His bare chest, now tanned, was wet and glistened in the afternoon sun. "Captain," the doctor shouted from the bow deck. "Please see to it the men drink enough water!" Rita Perez leaned over the rail next to him with a look of pity for the toiling souls.

"Girl," the Doctor requested, "Go to the galley and see if you can find sufficient salt to give each man a teaspoon when this ordeal is over." He put his hands on and bent over the rail. "Be off with you now, girl, and do as I say!" He scowled at her when she didn't move fast enough to suit him.

Mr. Cole walked up behind the Doctor and looked over his shoulder. "At least the Captain has gained the respect of the men over the past week of this valiant attempt against the sea."

"Indeed he has and that includes myself." The doctor stood up and turned. "How long before we change rowers?"

Cole pulled out his pocket watch and popped it open to glance at the time. "Thirty-five more minutes and my detachment will take over," he answered.

"Perhaps you could persuade him to postpone the next round until after sunset." the Doctor pleaded.

"I think not, Doctor. He'll want all the men on the same schedule, plus they rest better in the night air than during the heat of the day."

The Doctor looked to the sun high over head and masked his eyes with his left palm. "How far have we traveled, Mr. Cole?"

"Last shot put us nearly fifty miles farther south latitude than we were three days ago. Cole leaned over the rail and looked into the deeps of the water to mutter out a quiet prayer. "This weather just has to break and the winds return before we are entirely spent."

Morrison gently patted him on the back before he returned aft to his cabin and prepared to look after the exhausted men. As each day passed, it became more and more difficult to complete the four hour watch on the oars. Their desperation for the wind grew, but they persisted on, day after day, in what seemed like an endless struggle against nature.

Grafton's men were half way through the first shift of their twelfth day on the oars. They had taken a break to relieve themselves and drink a cup of water. Grafton was nearly spent himself and rested his head on the oar across his lap.

"Captain," Markell, the helmsman, grabbed him by the shoulder and shook him briskly. "Captain, look at the sails!" he cried. "They've started to fill, fill with the wind!" Two of the men across from Grafton hung their heads and began to cry.

Grafton made a raised fist over his head and shook his arm. "Yes!" He declared in triumph of his personal battle over the elements. "Let's get these boats back aboard men and become sailors again," he shouted to the other two craft.

By the time they got back to the side of the ship, the wind had completely filled the canvas. Bass Cole grabbed Grafton by the forearm to help him climb the last few feet to the deck. "Welcome aboard the sailing ship Bore Tide, Captain," he smiled. "I believe we are back in business."

"Stow these boats and set a course back toward the southwest Mr. Cole." He slapped him on the back and smiled, after he gained his footing on the deck. "And see to it these men get a double portion of rum with their meal tonight."

****

Mr. Cole was on the aft deck and in charge of sailing. He looked up to the sails, now filled and overflowing with wind which pushed the Bore Tide along at ten knots or better. The ship pounded in the waves and all was well with the world again. Joe Elder came up on deck to stand with Cole and enjoy the breeze. Before long they were joined by the Doctor and Major Bennett.

Two days had passed since the last shift of rowing and never would anyone have guessed that the sea could change so much in such a short time. Most of the crew had recovered from their intensive labor with the wooden paddles and were glad to be back to weapons training and meditation.

The Doctor looked around the deck at the bystanders. "Where's the Captain, Mr. Cole? He should be here to enjoy this glorious wind."

"There!" Cole pointed and raised his hand over his head to the top of the main mast above the crows nest.

"My God!" Bennett cried, horrified at the sight of a man who stood on the upper most yard arm of the topsail and leaned against the last section of mast. "What in the hell is he doing up there?"

"Enjoying the view and the only world he knows," Cole smiled. "Aboard ship, and for a man of the sea, it's a good place to think and work out your problems. I expect he'll be up there for some time."

The problem which so perplexed Captain Grafton was exactly what to do about a possible five million dollars worth of gold bullion not expected by his benefactor, Mr. Stepp.

CHAPTER VIII
THE HORN AND BEYOND

In the early morning light on 26 September, 1863, the southern lands of Argentina lay just off their starboard bow and the ship swung to the west to enter the open waters of Magellan's Passage. They were slightly ahead of schedule according to Grafton's calculations. The winds might not be as formidable and the water passages narrower, but the safety of this course far outweighed the dangers of the Horn's waters in Drake's Passage. His course decision also suited the mind set of his men.

Mr. Cole stood his watch on the aft deck, wearing his overcoat and large wool mittens. He pulled the collar of his jacket closer to his face, parched by the dry cold winds that swept over the deck. Several men of his watch scurried about the mid and forward decks to tend the lines and rigging. Major Bennett came up the steps from the officers' quarters and stood next to the shivering first officer.

"I guess the Captain decided to take the inside route after all, hey Mr. Cole." He said trying to make conversation and looked to the lands on both sides of the passage.

Cole looked over to his companion and snuggled his jacket collar even tighter about his face. "You must remember, Major," he shouted over the noise of the wind against the sail cloth. "That below 40 degrees latitude there is no law and below 50 degrees latitude there is no God!" He smiled and squinted his blue eyes into slits under his eyelids. "This is no place to take chances and the Captain is well aware of that fact."

"Interesting observation, Mr. Cole," he noted. "How long will it take us to round this land mass and start heading north?"

"Most likely we'll have to run against the wind this direction and the passage gets very narrow on the other end. We could even run out of wind altogether and have to row again." He shrugged his shoulders, "If we're lucky, maybe a week or so, maybe less."

"Is it better on the other side? I mean, in the Pacific Ocean?"

"We'll make our destination easily by mid November, which is well ahead of schedule I believe." The two men continued to stand for some time in silence while they watched the crew labor and listened

to the wind roar through the sails.
                                    ****

Though the weather had turned cooler outside, the bowels of the ship remained comfortable, in some places on the lower decks, below the cooking ovens, it was even hot. Rita Perez was off on a mission to search through a storage bin two decks below the crew quarters near the bow of the ship for a small barrel of salt pork. The light was extremely poor in the small compartment and hard for her to discern the different containers.

Harding and Masters had looked at each other across the table in the mess, when they overheard the old steward send the young black girl off on her errand. Sweat beaded on their foreheads and they were foul with soiled clothes from working in the cargo hold.

Both men had come to the mess for a break and coffee, but now in silent communication, both pondered the pleasures of the flesh the young lass could provide, willing or not. After she scurried out of the room, they got up one at a time and looked at the cook who labored over his stove as they passed.

The dim light poured through the open door of the storage bin and lit up the cream colored sailor's pants she wore. The door creaked and slowly rotated shut, which cut off the light. Startled, Rita turned to open it, but her hand touched the chest of a man instead. Before she could let out a sound, a massive dirty hand covered her face and mouth. He pushed her backward across several bags of rice and came to rest on top of her. He hurriedly pulled and struggled at her shirt, feeling her breasts under the cloth.

The door pushed open again and Harding turned his face into the light. The glow showed his frightened eyes and a sweaty face to the girl. The fear left him and he smiled in recognition of his partner, Masters. "There's plenty here for both of us," he growled and went back to his act of pawing her.

Masters sat down next to the girl and started to pull her pants toward her knees before he kicked the door shut. She struggled with the two more powerful men and tried to kick her way free, but it was no use. Harding swore and struggled with his own trousers to free himself. If was difficult to do and control the squirming girl under his body at the same time. Finally, he succeeded and forced his manhood into her body while she winced in pain.

Harding's hand slipped off her mouth and she let out a small scream before Master punched her face and threatened to kill her where she lay if she didn't remain silent. He held her shoulders and got excited while he watched his cohort continue to pump his body up and down into her feminine reaches. Harding finally groaned before he climaxed, and slumped over her exhausted, but Masters started to push at his shoulder to get him off for his turn.

"Hurry up for God's sake and get off of her before someone comes down here to look for her. I want my turn," he exclaimed, lying on his back as he desperately pulled at his own pants to expose his hardness. He managed to push Harding over and roll on top of the girl where he quickly took his partner's place. He shoved himself into the reaches of her body and pounded his own desires deep into the girl.

With a loud bang, the old wooden door burst open and slammed against the back bulkhead wall. The huge arm of Nelson Black came through the door to grab the back of Master's shirt and lift him off Rita. His manhood fully exposed, Nelson effortlessly threw him out the door and against the other side of the ship. Enraged at the sight of the helpless girl, Nelson turned out the door to plummet Masters for his transgression, but Harding was up off the floor before he realized it. With Black's attention diverted, Harding was able to pull a dagger from his waist belt and stab Nelson in the right side of his lower back.

Nelson fell into the opening on top of Masters and Harding jumped on his back. He raised the knife high over his head to finish the job on his victim. Rita screamed when she saw his arm start down with the knife, but her cries were covered by the report of a single gun shot. A bullet from Mr. Dobb's pistol passed completely through Harding's shoulder, splattering blood and fleshy matter across the bulkhead before it lodged into the wood.

Alerted by the cook of the suspicious nature of the two men's actions, Grafton ran up behind Dobbs in the close quarters. Smoky air filled the compartment from the pistol shot and his ears rang from the concussion. Dobbs knelt down and slowly rolled Nelson over. He coughed several times before he smiled and looked up at Dobbs. "I believe I owe you my life, what." He had no more gotten the words out of his mouth when he passed out. Several other crew members ran to the sound of the shot and now crowded the small space.

Grafton stepped over the two men and settled to one knee. He looked up to the others and ordered Doctor Morrison be summoned at once. "And get these two sons-of-bitches out of here," he said, with much aggravation, indicating Masters and Harding should go.

Within a short time, Doctor Morrison came hurrying down the hall with his bag and pulled Dobbs out of his way. He rolled Nelson over and examined the wound through the open slit in his shirt. His entire side was stained red with blood against the white cloth. Morrison placed gauze over the puncture and tied a strip of cloth around his waist. "Have some men get him up to my rooms," he said, with a grave look of concern at Grafton. He rose to walk away and knew his order would be obeyed.

Grafton pointed out two men to help and the three of them carried Nelson up to the deck with Rita following close on their heels. They spread him out on the wood table and rolled him up on his side so the Doctor could work. "Looks like the knife has punctured his kidney, maybe even the intestine." He shook his head and pushed the two sides of the wound together. He clenched his jaw and looked up at Grafton. "It doesn't look good Captain. I'll have to operate and see what kind of internal damage there is and if I can even repair it. The doctor paused, "He's probably already septic."

Mr. Cole burst into the room and looked horrified at the fallen black man. "Bring those two to the mid ship deck and assemble the men topside." Grafton ordered and glared from his bent over position. "I'll be there directly." Cole left to carry out his orders and Grafton looked over at Rita. "Are you all right, girl?" he asked.

She nodded her head yes with tears in her eyes and looked only to Nelson bleeding on the table. Grafton stood up and put a hand on her shoulder as he passed on his way out the door. "Do your very best for him, Doctor," he related but did not look back.

All of the crew gathered together and they were abuzz with the news of the girl's rape and a stabbing below decks. Dobbs, surrounded by the crew, now held the wounded Harding by the shoulder of his shirt to keep him from passing out on the deck. Masters was next to him with his hands tied behind his back. He shook with fright from the angry men and the cold wind.

Grafton came up onto the aft deck and looked down on the scene of men gathered below. "These two men took it upon themselves and felt they were free to rape our female guest. In doing so they attacked Mr. Black, who at this moment may well be dying below on the surgeon's table."

"I didn't stab anybody!" Masters cried.

"Shut your mouth before I hang you both from the yard arm." Grafton looked back to the crew. "These men are nothing but common criminals who prowl among you and wait for an opportunity to prey upon someone else."

"We wouldn't do that to the crew; these two are just a couple of nigger slaves." Harding tried to pull away from Dobbs defiantly as he screamed up at the Captain. "Where I come from they are nothing more than property, for Christ's sake, like a horse or cur dog and that's the way we treat them all." He smiled a cruel grin, "so what if I took my pleasure with that black bitch. That's why she was put here." Harding was so irate he was spitting out his words. "Giving her a poke is noth…

His vile words were cut short when Grafton drew his pistol with blinding speed and fired one shot at him from his elevated position. The bullet caught Harding just above his right eyelid and he slumped from the grasp of a startled Dobbs. His body fell to its knees and then twisted around and crumpled to the deck on its back.

Masters face grimaced when he looked down at the dead man. Tears began to flow out of his now tightly shut eyes because he knew what would be next. Grafton slowly cocked his pistol and moved the barrel to its new target. He held aim for several seconds and some of the men turned their heads. When Masters finally opened his eyes to a squint and looked up at his commander, Grafton de-cocked the weapon.

"Mr. Dobbs, take this man below to the keel and chain him to a bulkhead." Grafton placed the pistol back into the holster while he held his glare on Masters.

Masters body slumped in relief when Dobbs and two others took hold of him to remove him from the deck. He twisted around as they began to drag him away so he could see the Captain. "Thank you

Captain!" He shouted.

"Don't thank me yet, Masters. If Mr. Black dies, I'll still hang you." He turned to Mr. Cole on the aft deck. "Dismiss the men, if you please."

Cole shouted for the men to break up and return to their duties and ordered two others to prepare Harding's body for a sea burial. "We'll read over him tonight," he said nodding toward the body of the dead man. He watched while they picked him up from the deck and headed to the bow room. Cole then turned to Grafton who stood with his back to the crew.

"What do you intend to do with Masters if Nelson survives?" He asked.

Grafton took a deep breath and shook his head. "I don't know, and God knows we'll need every man if we run afoul of the French." He raised an eyebrow in thought. "But I can hardly let him off or the others will think they can have a go at the girl, too."

"I'm not so sure about that," Cole snorted, "after the example you just made with Harding."

"Perhaps you're right, Bass," he shrugged. "Harding has always been a snake of the lowest order and after what he did to Nelson it was a pleasure to dispatch him." He looked up to the wind filled sails. "Let's keep on course and see if we can get through this passage without further problems." He started down the stairs to the mid deck. "You have the helm, Mr. Cole. I am going to check on Nelson."

Cole watched him walk around the blood pool that stained the mid-deck on his way forward and he stopped one of the crew. "Get this mess cleaned up will you." He said and pointed to the puddle of blood.

****

For the most part, the wind held and the ship made the rest of the passage without significant problems. Only once did the men have to put out the long boats to pull the craft around a jetty on the lee side of the wind. Other than that, the sails remained full. Only five days saw them free and clear to maneuver in the Pacific Ocean on their way north to Baja.

Doctor Morrison had operated twice on Nelson and he had yet to regain complete consciousness. Luckily for him, the blade was narrow and didn't do a lot of damage. It had sliced the upper right kidney and nicked his intestine. The Doctor was very concerned because over the past several hours his temperature had been rising and he began to convulse. Rita stayed at his side constantly from the start and refused to leave, or even sleep.

Morrison sent urgent word late on the fifth night for Grafton to come at once to the dispensary. He made his way through the darkened ship to the surgeon's door and pushed it open. "What is it Doctor?" he asked, with concerned voice.

Morrison looked from Grafton to his patient and picked up his arm to take his pulse. "I'm afraid he's dying and there isn't much left I can do."

"There must be something Doctor," Grafton quietly urged, "You just can't quit on him now."

"I fear he has this fever from the intestine puncture and his body is fighting very hard to ward off any infection. That is why his temperature is so high and it is also the reason it will kill him. His heart won't take much more of this overload." Morrison shrugged and looked back at Grafton with sadness in his eyes. "I've seen this before, I am sorry," he said and placed Nelson's arm back on the table.

"Kill or cure," Rita softly said while she rubbed Nelson's other arm and tears filled her eyes.

"What did you say?" Morrison asked.

"It's an ancient treatment for a high fever," she said and looked at the two men. "You douse a body in chilling cold water then wrap them in a wet wool blanket until the fever breaks." She looked at their amazement. "The problem is, most times the cold water is too much for the heart and it kills. But if he can stand the shock it will also let his body cure the infection. They call it kill or cure."

"It just might work," the Doctor said after some reflection. I've used that technique of a quick douse on babies with high fevers but never adults, and never for a sustained period." Morrison tipped his head. "He's damn sure dead if we do nothing."

Several men hauled buckets of bone chilling sea water up from the side of the ship and dumped them over Black's nude body laid out on deck while the doctor supervised. In his convulsive state he screamed out with pain and shivered with the chills from the dousing.

After several minutes they pulled him from the deck and rolled his body into several wet wool blankets.

Within thirty minutes his temperature had dropped considerably and the shaking had stopped. The Doctor knelt next to him to check his status continually and finally looked up to Grafton and the other crewmembers. "His convulsions are over and his heart rate is back to normal." He looked down at Rita who was soaking wet on her knees next to him. "He's just sleeping now, girl," Morrison smiled. "You may have just saved his life." He motioned to the crew. "Let's get him dried and back to sick bay."

By late morning Black was conscious, talkative and on the mend thanks to the cold water. Everyone seemed pleased at the sudden turn of events, especially Gordon Masters, still shackled to the lower bulkhead.

Five days after Black's near death experience, Grafton had the crew assembled again on deck, then ordered Masters brought up from below. Dobbs unshackled the man and pushed him from behind, forward in front of the other men.

"You are a lucky man." Grafton began to speak from the aft deck with a whip in his hand. "I would be well within my rights as Captain to hang you for your offense. However, I suppose Harding has already paid the greater price so I have decided to commute your sentence of death. At the same time I cannot allow your acts to go unpunished. Therefore, you will kiss the gunner's daughter." Grafton looked to his most senior crew member and ship's gunner, Joseph Flanders, who stood among the men. "Your mates will punish you."

"Mr. Cole, give Mr. Flanders this whip and he will administer punishment for the entire crew." Grafton pointed out several other men. "Tie him over the cannon gentlemen and strip his back bare." While the men carried out his command, Grafton continued. "Mind you now the gravity of his offense and see to it that you do not share the same fate."

Mr. Cole handed Flanders the whip, who had a look of remorse on his face over the task at hand. Even so, he dutifully walked over to the cannon where Masters was now sprawled out. The old crewman pulled a belay from the rail and stuck it in Master's mouth, then stood in silence behind the man, looking at the whip. He thought about what he'd been ordered to do and readied himself for the task.

"Fifteen lashes if you please, Mr. Flanders," Grafton commanded. When the old man didn't immediately start, he added, "Smartly now."

The whip snapped with contact to Masters' back and all the men on deck winced at the noise each time that awful crack reached their ears. By the fourth count Masters' back began to bleed but he held his tongue and did not cry out.

Sweat peppered his forehead and his jaw chomped down hard on the hickory stick in his mouth as he took heavy breaths through his nose. Every time the leather stung his back his eyes squeezed shut, still he did not cry out. At long last the final blow was struck and some of the men rushed forward to release him from the cannon.

Masters stood to his feet and pushed the others away, swaying, barely able to maintain his balance. With great difficulty he managed to turn around and face his Captain. Masters stood on wobbly legs with a defiant look on his face, still breathing heavily through his mouth.

Grafton reached into his sash to pull out a ten dollar gold piece and flipped it to Masters who caught it in mid air. "I salute your bravery, Sir, not to have cried out and to have taken your punishment as a man should have." He looked to Morrison. "Get this man below, Doctor, and see to his injuries. He is to be returned to duty when able and we shall not speak of this again. The matter is closed."

****

They continued north over a thirty day period while Nelson grew stronger by the hour. Before they rounded the top shoulder of South America he was again his old self, laughing, enjoying life and training the men for their mission, though with less vigor.

All of that was going well too. Several of the men had become rather proficient with the Gatling guns and enjoyed firing such a magnificent and deadly weapon. Their hand to hand combat skills greatly improved by now, thanks to Grafton, Black and Elder. These three men had come to respect each other's ability with weapons and their personal fighting skills. The time of confrontation drew near and everything began to fall into place.

The officers had just finished their evening meal and departed the mess when Grafton stopped Dobbs at the door. "Have Mr. Flanders brought up here to my quarters."

"Yes, Sir," he paused. "May I inquire as to if he is in some trouble with you, Captain? He'll surely ask."

"Certainly not," he smiled. "Fetch him here if you please."

The old man knocked before he entered the Captain's cabin. It was a place most sailors never got close to and, for a crewman, it's about as intimidating a place as there ever was on board ship. "You sent for me, Captain?" he asked, wringing his tam in his hands.

Grafton looked up at the old man with long dirty thinning silver hair and unkempt clothes. He was in desperate need of a shave but did not yet have a beard. For his size he looked bone tough with no spare flab anywhere and under the outward appearance was the long lost face of a handsome younger man. "You served in the Queen's Navy, did you not?" Grafton asked.

"Ah, yes Sir, twenty six years, Sir. Gunners mate to gunner master under many a Captain, Sir."

"Perhaps then you could explain what it is that we seem to be doing wrong on our cannon practice and why the men can't get off more than one or two shots." Grafton raised an eyebrow. "Well, Mr. Flanders, what is your opinion?"

"Wrong, Sir," he paused. "I'd say just about everything, Sir."

Grafton continued to stare at the old man in silence and watched him shift his weight until he realized the Captain wanted an explanation.

"You need to move some of your powder supply up between the guns so it's close by, along with the shot. We used to have little boys run supplies. You also need two more men on each gun station to roll it out faster and to help water down after the shot itself. As soon as it hits the stop, the wick should be put to the flame and it all needs to be done on the roll of the ship. That is, if you want to hit a frigate from a modified brig and not sink her." He smiled.

"Anything else?"

"Why yes, Sir, you need one man in command of all the guns on each deck to say when and how everything is done during the fight."

"Would you like to be that man, Flanders?" Grafton asked.

"I'd be honored, Sir, but that task should fall to an officer." He grinned.

Grafton stood, poured two glasses of Port without any response to his protest, and handed one to Flanders. "If we are to take on the French, we will need to bring her and the crew down as quickly as possible without, as you surmised, hulling the ship. If I can get you really close before any cannon fire is exchanged, what would be our best course of action?"

He took the drink and gulped it all down much to Grafton's amusement. "Not too close now Captain, cause we're smaller and we'll have to shoot upwards on a roll or you'll never take her." He paused and cleared his throat from the stiff drink. "Chains, Captain. In the old days we used to have the blacksmith make up two balls from the six pounders, one heavier than the other, tied together with four or five feet of chain." He smiled broadly. "Never knew where the buggers would hit swapping ends for ends on their merry way. But I tell you this; they played bloody hell with a ship's rigging. I've even seen'em bring down a frigate's main mast."

"That's interesting, Mr. Flanders."

"Split the guns between double balls, straight chains and grape shot." He nodded his head. "That will stop her in her tracks and don't worry about the crew. Those fancy spitting guns up there on deck will take care of them."

Grafton pulled the door to his cabin open and hollered for Mr. Cole who came down from the upper deck. "Mr. Flanders will have complete control of any further cannon training performed by the crew. Mr. Elder will be relieved from that duty as of tomorrow." Grafton looked back to Flanders. "If we are involved in any sea action against the French, he will have absolute control of cannon firing. Anyone not in support of a Gatling gun will learn and assist Mr. Flanders on cannons." He paused while Cole awaited further orders.

"Mr. Dobbs will learn the fine art of being a cannon master so he may assist Flanders on the lower deck," the Captain shrugged. "Is there anything else Mr. Flanders?" he asked.

"No Sir. By the end of the week I'll have those boys ready to take on those Frogs like we did in the old days." Flanders came to attention and snapped his arm up as if he were saluting a British Naval Officer before he walked out of the room, now with the step of a much younger man.

Grafton smiled at Cole. "I believe I added several years to his life just now, Bass." His grin disappeared. "I just wish I had known of his expertise some weeks ago so we could have been better prepared with our cannon." Grafton returned to his chart table and began to study the coast. "See to it that he gets whatever he requires," he said without looking up.

CHAPTER IX
BAJA AND BETRAYAL

Summer heat returned to the Bore Tide with a vengeance and Grafton, along with the rest of the crew, had trouble with sleep. Naps were about the best he could muster these days and he became annoyed when someone woke him, like now, with a knock on his cabin door.

"Enter!" he shouted.

His steward quickly pushed open the hatch. "Land, Captain, the southern tip of California, I believe.

Grafton partially dressed and made his way to the deck where he found Mr. Cole glassing the horizon off the starboard bow.

Cole heard the Captain's footsteps but did not look back from his scan. "Fifty nine days fourteen hours from Jamaica." He snapped the glass shut. "I guess your little rowing exhibition really paid off. This should give us plenty of time to set our trap for the French and maybe even stave off any hostilities."

"We can but hope, Mr. Cole," Grafton replied and strained his eyes over the bow to better see the land mass ahead. "Follow the Baja Peninsula north to La Paz, then we'll strike northeast to the town of Bahio Kino." He stretched his body with a hold on the front rail and pushed backwards while he thought out loud to Mr. Cole. "That is where the trade is to take place, but we must also be careful not to stumble into the Confederate Army there."

"There is no way they could arrive any time soon even if that General left the same day we did." Cole pushed his cap back on his head and scratched his scalp. "He'd still be hundreds of miles from here." he paused. "Wouldn't he?"

"You forget Mr. Cole, he, like us, must also wait for the French. That will give the General a chance to amass his forces on the coast and push us into a sea battle. We can but hope the French arrive first and it is they who must wait." The two men walked over to the deck map and stood in front of the helm. Grafton opened the top and rolled out the map.

"Mr. Elder, Major Bennett and I, along with a small contingent of men which will also include Ms. Perez, who is fluent in Spanish, will go ashore. We will try to ascertain any information we can from the populace." He moved his finger on the map north to the Island of Isla Tiburon. "You will move the ship to a safe harbor here and hide. We will take the portable heliograph to communicate and I want you to keep at least two men in the crows nest around the clock to watch for our signals and the harbor for the French."

Cole turned his head and looked over Grafton's shoulder at the map to the location he'd indicated. "If the French should arrive, we won't stand much of a chance with you and the others off the ship and in those close waters."

"Bass, I think the French are the only ones we can depend on to be on time or even a little late." Grafton turned and leaned back against the table, knowing the helmsman also listened. "I have been concerned this whole time that something is wrong and we do not have the right information on the timing of General Applegate's intentions. Therefore we will not put in at Bahio Kino. Instead my party will go ashore in a long boat and you will continue on to the island and wait."

"A trap, perhaps?" he asked.

"Or worse, there could be a traitor in our midst." Grafton raised an eyebrow. "In any case, have Mr. Dobbs set the guns and cannons on his watch as soon as you make berth. Issue the men their arms so they can be ready at a moment's notice."

"As you wish, Captain," Cole replied. "I estimate we should be at Bahio Kino by late in the afternoon day after tomorrow."

"From here on, Mr. Cole, keep a sharp eye and a clear head."

****

Nine men were aboard the launch that oared away from the Tide as she made sail to the north. The port town of Bahio Kino seemed quiet enough from a distance and no ships of any kind were in the small harbor. The southern reaches of the Isla Tiburon, where Cole would hide the ship, was easily seen with the naked eye from the outskirts of town. As the boat neared the shore, several old men dressed in white cloth began to wave from below two sod adobe buildings which stood just above the tide line. It appeared to be a desperately poor village with few people.

"Make to those men," Grafton indicated to the helmsman and pointed out the pair on the beach. "We'll soon find out what they know."

Elder jumped from the front of the small launch, splashing into the light surf, and secured the boat to the sand while the others got out. The locals wandered up to the strangers now on the beach and shouted words of welcome. Perez moved to the front and made the first contact.

After a short conversation she told the Captain that the town welcomed the strangers and offered meals and drinks for all. They also were curious why the great ship left the shore and did not stop.

"Rita, please extend my gratitude to this committee for their hospitality and generous offer of food and drink which we will be glad to accept." He paused in thought. "Tell them that I am the Captain of the great ship and need their assistance before it can return to this harbor. Tell them we have many gifts for the people of this village on the ship."

Perez raised an eyebrow but translated the message as the Captain had spoken it. In short order, all of the men were headed to a small cantina in the center of the one street town. Several children followed along and some women watched from open doors as they proceeded down the street. Upon entering the building, the men fanned out into the small room of the cantina and seated themselves at various tables. Grafton sat with the unofficial greeters and Perez.

He removed his cap and slid up close to the table. "Ask these gentlemen if they know anything about an army detachment in the vicinity or heard rumors of pending trouble here about." He sat quietly while Perez carried on a rather lengthy conversation and shifted uneasily in her chair.

She pushed back with a forlorn look. "I take it by your demeanor and conversation that there is some brew of trouble in the area?" Grafton asked.

"Mr. Mendez here," she tipped her open hand to the smiling older man across the table who nodded his head. "He said a runner arrived yesterday with news of a great body of men, Americans they think, which march in this direction from Santa Ana. He says the town is frightened and that the runner left for Chihuahua just this morning to alert the Mexican authorities. He says the Army is in Mexico City and would not get here for many months. That is why he wants to know if we came to save them."

"Those hills to the north," Grafton noted. "Is there someone in town who can show us the best way up there and see this body of men for ourselves?"

After a short conversation, Perez turned and answered. "Yes, he says his grandson can take us."

"Tell the old man his people have nothing to fear from the army. Tell him they come to meet a French ship, then will go away." Grafton told her. "Tell him they are not his enemy."

After the conversation, Perez just shook her head. "He said that the Federalies will not be pleased with the American's presence and should they come, they will fight. He asks if we can make them go away before the war comes to his little village."

A girl brought drinks and tortillas to the table and set a dirty glass of mescal in front of Grafton. He held it up to look through it and grimaced before he smiled at her hospitality. Without taking his eyes off the girl, he answered, "Tell him the French ship will not come so the army will go home before they have to fight the Federalist troops."

Elder looked at Grafton with serious eyes because he knew exactly what that omen foretold. After lunch, the old man's grandson showed up on the dirty street with several burros and two mules for their journey. The men unloaded the launch with the supplies and two local boys helped load the materials. The younger Mendez spoke relatively good English and said the trip would take the rest of the day and late into the night. He also suggested that they be ready to observe early in the morning before heat made everything far away impossible to see.

They took with them the heliograph, a large telescope on a tripod, some food and lots of water, which, according to their guide, was non-existent beyond the town and all the way into the hills. The trip proved extremely difficult due to the sagebrush and thorns, which no one was used to and was made even worse by the incessant heat. Joe Elder, it seemed to Grafton, was finally at home and walked with a renewed vigor.

The party reached the tallest of three hills near midnight under a full moon. They set up camp below the summit to keep the fires out of sight of any forward elements. Grafton and the others had suffered all day in the heat but now felt they were about to freeze to death on the wind swept hill. He sensed it was hostile country and could be an enemy to man all in itself.

A breeze fluttered the clothing of the men huddled around the fire while they drank coffee and complained about blistered feet. Grafton threw the last of his cold coffee into the fire and announced he would try and sleep until dawn. He wandered a short distance and spread out a wool blanket next to a fallen log, where he covered himself and tried to gain some comfort in the sand.

Elder came over and sat on the log to finish his drink. "Do you think we will see the Confederate Army in the morning?" he asked in a muted tone.

"If we do," Grafton replied from under the blanket without looking out, "we have a spy in our midst that provided bad information all around." Elder stood and looked at the man under the blanket before he drew a long breath and returned to the warmth of the fire.

"Damn," Grafton whispered under his breath as he looked through the glass in the grey morning light from the top of the craggy hill. "It's them alright," he said and looked back at Elder with the knowing eye of his earlier comment. He went back to his observation. "Odd," he commented, "looks like an extremely culled down brigade. I'd say no more than 300 men with 15 or so wagons and fifty extra horses."

"There is no way Applegate could possibly be this far along with that size force and not have left before we were in Richmond." Bennett said, while he looked over Grafton's shoulder with his binoculars. "But how could it be we managed to get those papers?" He asked quizzically and looked back at Elder.

"We didn't," Grafton looked up from the telescope. "I thought it was too easy. They knew we would be there and what we were after. Even if we beat the general here, the French would slaughter us when we presented the wrong document. Or perhaps," he stopped in thought, "if the army had been a few days earlier they would have captured us on the beach." He stopped talking out loud and studied a scorpion on his boot, "But of course, I should have thought of it before!"

"Who betrayed us?" Bennett said still holding his glasses up while he looked down at Grafton.

"Who indeed, Major?" Grafton stood so Elder could have a look at the sight through the glass. "The sooner we find the answer to that question, the better off we will be." He shouted down the backside of the hill and told Perez to tell the bearers to pack up the mules and bring up the heliograph.

Elder studied the formation for a moment in silence before he commented, "I'd say two, maybe three days and they'll be in the town. We should be especially careful on the way back that we do not stumble into any forward elements. They could be most anywhere." He sounded worried.

Grafton set up the heliograph while the porters watched in amazement at the strange instrument. He adjusted its position and glanced up at the rising sun. "Spin the telescope around toward the island out there in the bay."

Elder brought it around and adjusted the aperture, "What am I looking for? he asked.

Grafton began clicking out a series of flashes, then stopped. From his position he didn't need the telescope to see the return light flash from the ship. Elder turned his head and squinted his eyes from the blinding light in the scope. "Aren't you afraid everyone in the entire country will see that?"

"Line of sight only, so it is relatively safe unless someone is between us and the ship and then they would have to understand the code to know what is being said." Grafton spoke while he tapped out his message. When he finished, he began to re-box his toy with the help of the porters. "Let's get back to the ship with haste and get out of here." He paused and looked back to the direction of the army, "I don't want to run into them or their units even by accident."

By late afternoon the small caravan approached the outskirts of the village, nearly done in by the forced march across the scrub. Young Mendez suddenly stopped his burro on the dusty road to study his home town. Grafton and Elder pulled up, too. "Seems too quiet, doesn't it?"

"Si," the young man nodded and listened intently. Elder slowly withdrew his pistol and cocked it as did Bennett. Grafton looked back at his men and hand signaled them to get out their weapons. He then pulled a repeater rifle off the burro himself and checked the action. "You and the town's men stay here with the equipment, son," Grafton ordered, without looking at the boy, and started forward.

The others followed their Captain and began to fan out as they cautiously approached the first buildings. They worked their way ever farther into the center of town, but the eerie quiet, heat and stress ground on the men's nerves. Grafton saw an old man hoeing some flowers in the town square next to the communal well and their eyes met. He slowly looked to the church door across the square and slightly nodded.

Grafton fired two quick successive shots at the door and a Confederate soldier stumbled out into the light, holding his chest before he fell to the ground. More shots rang out as Grafton's men ducked for cover and began to shoot back. The fighting only lasted a couple of minutes because the Confederates only had muskets against the repeater rifles.

A white flag pushed out from the top of the church steeple and Grafton hollered for his men to stop firing. When the rifle shots subsided, he slowly stood, exposing himself to the enemy in the building. A young officer followed by three men came out the front door with their weapons held over their heads. Elder, Grafton and the men approached and encircled the survivors.

"Is this everyone?" Grafton asked the lieutenant.

"Yes, Sir," he nodded. "You managed to kill the other seven."

"Mr. VanDorn," Grafton turned to look at one of his crewmen behind him. "Do we have any losses?"

"Kelvin is dead, Sir, shot through the forehead and Fitzgerald has a minor arm wound. Otherwise we're in good shape," he answered. "You gonna kill this bunch so we can be on our way."

"Shoot'em for killing, Kelvin, Captain," several of the men demanded. "We can't leave them here anyway."

The young lieutenant nervously looked at the men who surrounded him and flinched when Grafton pulled the man's sword from its scabbard. He held it up and examined it in the sunlight. "This is a fine weapon and even has your name, Sandoval of Mobile, engraved on the shank. That is your name, no?" Grafton asked, twisting the blade high in the air.

The lieutenant nodded but did not answer and Grafton lowered the sword touching the point into the flesh on Sandoval's neck. "Swear to me on the honor of the family Sandoval of Mobile that you and your men will not attempt to escape or in any way interfere with our mission while in our company. He pushed the point harder, "On your word as a gentleman, Sir."

"I swear it, Sir." He replied.

Grafton lowered the tip and flipped the sword around to present the handle to the somewhat stunned lieutenant. "You may keep your sword, Sir, but I will have that side arm." The lieutenant pushed his sword back into its sheath and unbuttoned the holster to hand over his handgun.

"Now I don't have to worry about you," he smiled. "VanDorn," Grafton shouted. "Go and fetch our supplies and Miss Perez so we can depart in the long boat. And detail these southern gentlemen to bury Mr. Kelvin and their comrades before we leave. He turned and looked back at Sandoval. "Are there any more of your kind lurking about?"

"I agreed not to escape or interfere in your business, Sir, not provide you with information," the lieutenant insisted.

"Yes," Grafton smiled, "you did." He patted the young man on the shoulder for his sense of duty. "Search him, Mr. Elder, and the others as well, including the dead."

****

It was early evening when Captain Grafton climbed the side of the Bore Tide and the sun was just beginning to sink below the low hills of the island. Mr. Cole met him on the deck. He looked to the head mast and the fluttering Dutch flag. "As soon as everything is aboard, Mr. Cole, get us underway and out of this inlet."

"Yes, Sir, we are ready to sail."

"Very well. Get us down the channel and out to sea, then start a tack course to find the French." He took a long breath and solemnly looked at his first officer. "Our hand has been forced into a fight for the cargo. I'll tell the crew myself in the morning and we'll start final preparations."

Grafton started to his cabin then stopped to look back at Cole, "Have the cook make sure everyone gets a hot meal with double rations."

CHAPTER X
THE FRENCH FRIGATE
AND GOLD

The officers and guests sat around Grafton's mess table while the steward poured glasses of port. They had cleared lands end and now searched for the French ship along coastal waters. Grafton pulled an envelope from his pocket, but waited until the steward left before he handed it to Mr. Martrovich. "Our Richmond prize," he paused. "Please," he motioned with his up turned palm. "Open it and read aloud to the group."

Martrovich shifted in his chair uneasily, but did as was requested. He shook out the paper and cleared his throat before he started. "To the representatives of the Southern States of the Confederacy and President Jefferson Davis, we of the French National Diplomatic Service, direct representatives of King Louis the III of France, do hereby grant to the great American Confederate Nation the sum of fifteen million U.S. dollars in gold bullion for support in the cause of liberty in which your country is now engaged. This sum will be transferred to the duly appointed military authority bearing this document at the location specified in earlier negotiations and between the parties specified by each government."

Martrovich waved his hand over the document, "Signed by the representatives of the king and so forth and so on." He looked up. "My French isn't perfect, but that's the general drift of the instrument."

Major Bennett was stunned at the amount while Elder just whistled. Grafton looked over the group. "I made a deal with Undersecretary Nathan Stepp to deliver ten million in gold bullion and that is exactly what I intend to do."

"Now wait just a minute!" Bennett shouted in a loud voice. "That money is the property of the United States."

"No, it is not, Sir. That money belongs to the Confederacy and to us when and if we manage to take it away from the French."

Doctor Morrison set his wine glass down, "You are rather cavalier about this matter, aren't you, Captain, considering the Union might not see this situation the same way you do. Speaking as a military officer, I should think they will hang you for theft!"

"Both of you gentlemen are free to explain the situation to Secretary Stepp should we be lucky enough to return to Washington." Grafton took a sip from his glass, "I am willing to take my chances." He shrugged, "Who knows, maybe you'll be one of the lucky men to return here to recover it, Major."

Grafton and Cole exchanged a knowing glance. "You're not even going to take it back to Washington?" Bennett questioned.

"No, I'm not, Major. I have told you about this in the event something happens to either Mr. Cole or I. If by some chance the gold doesn't get returned, it will become the stuff of legends and future generations will argue over its location for a millennium. I can think of no better way for the Bore Tide, or us, to be remembered in history."

"Or you'll just come back and steal it later," the Major grumbled.

"Steal is a very strong word, Major. I prefer to think of it as a recovery. Besides," he smiled, "we'll put it to a very good use." Grafton look up before he took a breath. "There is another option you gentlemen might care to consider."

"Something we missed?" Bennett huffed out.

"There is more than enough gold to go around for all here." He paused and utter silence fell over the room. "Haven't you ever wanted to be rich Bennett, with servants at your beck and call, nice clothes, mansions and luxury all around? Or you doctor, your own clinic and hospital and all those government grants. Mr. Elder here could buy into the railroads that will be built after the war and become a shipping magnate."

"You are a corrupting bastard, that's for damn sure, Captain," Elder blurted out.

"A common thief is more like it," the Major added.

Grafton sat up straight in his chair. "I am anything but a common thief, Major. I am an exceptional thief and a pirate. You said so yourself." He let the idea of larceny settle on the humid air of the cabin before he cleared his throat. "There will be time to reflect about these events until we find the French and decide what course we are all willing to take. Perhaps they will settle this question and send us to the bottom."

****

The Captain had mustered the men to the center deck to confirm the news that scuttle butt had already made clear. There would indeed be a battle with the French and now was the time to make the necessary preparations. Grafton had kept the ship crossing the Baja straight and two men on look out above at all times. The cannons were loaded and the Gatling guns primed and covered with tarps. Each day the men drilled at their positions and assignments. All that remained was a modicum of luck and to find the French ship.

Grafton also informed the men he did not want any of the French officers killed after they boarded the ship, which brought a roar of displeasure. If they were to be captured, he explained, they could be made to surrender and stop the fighting. The quicker the better and all agreed.

Ten days out of Bahio Kino the look out shouted the word that a sailing ship was sighted on the horizon. Grafton changed course and colors. He had Mr. Dobbs bring out a small surprise; a French flag to hoist to the top sail. He watched the ship grow larger in his glass until he confirmed it was the Paris De Sal, their bounty.

"Steady as she goes, Mr. Cole," Grafton said while he continued to track the ship in his glass. "They don't seem to be arming up and her gun ports are still closed." He slammed his glass shut. "Two points to port when we get within 100 yards so the ship will roll in the swells Mr. Cole, and we can bring down her mainsails."

Grafton stepped up to the poop deck rail and shouted, "Mr. Flanders whatever you do, I implore you not to hull that ship!"

"Understood, Sir," he shouted back. "But we'll make'em wish they'd stayed in France." He smiled at the thought of battling his old adversaries.

"Very good, Mr. Flanders," Grafton turned to watch the frigate grow larger and he could hear his own heart pound in his chest, frightened at the unknown variables of battle. He could now see men on the upper deck lined up to watch the approach of another French ship.

Cole turned at the hip to the helmsman, "Two points to port, Mr. Markell." Grafton put his head down and whispered under his breath as the two ships came along side of each other. "Wait for the roll, Mr. Flanders."

"Fire!" he screamed and eight cannon erupted on the starboard deck. Thunder, smoke and screams filled the air along with wood splinters flying in every direction. The men assigned to the Gatling guns quickly pulled down the tarps and the relentless pops of fire sounded from both ends of the Tide. Men fell and holes magically appeared in the side of the frigate. The cracking sound of breaking wood was everywhere.

Two cannons fired into the Bore Tide and the side just above the first deck broke away, killing several men below. Flanders was ready when the ships rolled apart and he fired a second volley. This time the main mast splintered and fell from the frigate across the Bore Tide, bringing down sails and spars from both ships. The rear Gatling gun tore into all crew members on deck and they fell in great numbers, while the other two continued to wreck destruction on the lower decks of the ship.

As soon as Flanders fired the third volley, Grafton gave the signal to throw out the grappling hooks and board the French ship. When the first men began to swing and jump between the ships, most gun fire ceased. Mr. Black and several other men were at the Captain's side when they dropped down into the chaos on the deck. The Frenchmen attacked them immediately with swords and clubs, but Grafton made his way aft, cutting down several sailors with his sword as he went. The sounds of rifle fire intensified as more of his crew came aboard.

Grafton got into a sword fight with a junior officer at the bottom of the poop deck steps, which nearly cost him his life. The man was more than an excellent swordsman and managed to disarm Grafton. The officer was about to stab him to death as he fell back trying to draw his pistol, but before the blade touched him a shot rang out and the officer fell dead to the deck.

Grafton got up and spun around to see who had saved him. Ten feet further down the deck stood Masters, still holding the smoking rifle. He nodded at his captain before he racked the lever for another shot. Grafton picked up his saber and ran up the steps behind Black and together, they disarmed a senior officer.

The man stumbled back and fell against the rail. Grafton put the tip of his sword on the officer's chest. "Your pardon, Sir," he demanded.

He nodded in agreement, with a look of disgust on his face over being taken, but reversed his sword and handed it to Grafton.

"Your captain," Grafton said in French. "Tell him to surrender his ship!

"You have killed my captain," the officer explained in broken English." He stood from the rail, calmly walked forward and shouted down for the others to stop the fight. Ever so slowly fighting and gun fire subsided. When it quieted, he turned to Grafton, "Who are you? And what is it you want?"

He looked at the officer, then his two dead comrades crumpled on the deck, and did not answer his question, but instead went forward to search out Mr. Cole. "Masters," he shouted. "Where is Mr. Cole?"

"I believe he went below, Sir." Masters turned to look over the mess on the upper deck and the men being held under arms. "What should we do with these men?" he asked.

"Put all the survivors up on the bow deck and transfer all wounded back to the Tide for Doctor Morrison." Grafton looked over the dead men. "How many are ours, Mr. Masters?"

"Two or three," he glumly said and looked around. "Maybe more below or on the Tide."

Grafton spied Doctor Morrison on the upper deck of the Tide and shouted to him from the rail. "How many, Doctor?"

"Six dead and five wounded over here the best I can tell right now. Two of the confederate men are among them."

Nelson Black smiled at Grafton and patted him on the shoulder. "It was a good battle, Alexander, and a good day. I guess we shall survive, shant we."

Grafton nodded but looked back to the Doctor. "Stay there and we'll rig a sling to send the wounded over to you." Grafton turned when he heard Cole run up behind him.

He was out of breath but managed to get it out. "We found it, Sir! Down in the middle hold in hundred pound crates and damn it's full!" He took a deep breath, "The men know, Sir."

Grafton smiled, "Never knew any secret that could be kept." He reached out and put his hand on Cole's shoulder. "Get that rigging cleared off the Tide and I'll see to our damage. Let's get tied off so we can transfer the wounded and rig a sling to move the gold." He looked back at the French officer. "Put him forward with his men."

Cole turned and indicated to the officer he should come with him.

"My men are being cared for, yes?" he asked.

Grafton stepped up and handed him his sword. "You are the Captain of this vessel now and you'll need this when we depart."

The Frenchman reached out to take his sword. "You and your men will be humanely treated and the wounded cared for, Captain. Once we secure the ship you may bury your dead." Grafton informed him.

Within an hour, the fallen rigging was cleared away and pushed over board, all of the wounded were below being treated and Grafton had surveyed the damage to the Tide. Several large holes were shot completely through the ship, four feet above the water line, and the forward hold was useless because of it. The gold was in the process of being transferred.

Eleven of his men lay dead and nine were wounded, two badly. One of the Confederate enlisted men had been hit by a stray bullet and succumbed to the wound. The French were binding dead bodies on the deck of their ship for burial and everyone was too occupied to give other matters much thought at the moment. Grafton was pushing wood out a large hole below decks when he heard steps behind him and looked up.

"Glad to see you well, Mr. Dobbs." He smiled. "You must be relieved to have it over with."

"Indeed, Captain," he nodded and swallowed. "Ship's company is down to twenty three able-bodied men and one woman. We have three prisoners and twelve French wounded aboard, with no spare men to watch them." He paused and looked around at the mess in the hold before he continued his report, while the Captain fidgeted about. "The frigate was grossly under manned for her size, which was lucky for us, and well over half her guns have been removed. We killed forty-two of her crew and five officers," he sadly reflected.

"Obviously they weren't expecting trouble and she probably isn't commissioned as a war ship any longer in any case." Grafton observed. "I noticed the Frenchmen are not military men." He stood up from his labors and dropped a piece of siding plank. "Send that Confederate Officer to my quarters, Mr. Dobbs," he said and walked around his second mate toward the forward door.

"Lieutenant Sandoval," Grafton said, with his back to the young lieutenant when he came in his cabin. Grafton was washing up at a table in the back. He turned and picked up a towel, drying his hands and faced the man. "We are in the process of unloading that French ship and when we're finished I intend to scuttle it," he said and threw the towel down on the table."

"So why tell me?" He asked.

"I am short of crew and in need of men. I realize neither you nor your two remaining men are sailors. However, there are duties to which you could be useful while we sail and I thought perhaps you may have had enough of fighting a lost cause and would care to join us."

"I hardly consider the Confederacy a lost cause and I am an officer, Sir, not prone to become a traitor and I consider this offer an insult," he scoffed.

Grafton observed the man for a moment who likely sought an apology. "Of course," he said at last. "I'll waste no man to watch you. The remaining Frenchmen will be set adrift in their launches with food and water along with maps and compass. If their officer is any kind of sailor he should find the coast in two or three day's time. If he is not, it is likely to be a long winter for you because you will be with them."

"You're setting us free, then?" he asked in amazement.

"If you can call it that." Grafton sat down at his desk. "Look Lieutenant, tell that Frenchman to make for Bahio Kino where your general is most likely at by now and you'll have a good chance to survive. If he goes directly to the coast, you will find yourselves some two hundred miles south of your forces in hostile country with bandits and Federales under every rock, ready to slit your collective throats."

****

"By five in the afternoon, the gold was moved aboard, all the rigging was cleared and the two ships were ready to be cut apart. Mr. Dobbs had surveyed the launches on the frigate and found six of them to be sea worthy. He had some men lower the boats and set stores for a journey. He found maps, compass and sextant in the Captain's quarters and put those aboard as well. Mr. Cole set a scuttle charge in the bilge with three barrels of gun powder and fuses. The French were now sliding their dead into the sea, one man at a time, while Grafton watched from the deck.

When they finished he approached the new Captain. "We have put everything you need in the launches for a trip to shore," he informed the solemn officer. "You should make for Bahio Kino where you will find a friendly town and probably the Confederate Army. Do not attempt to return to this ship." Grafton started to turn away, but stopped.

"By the way, you will be taking the three of them with you," he smiled and pointed to the forward cabin. "Let your men collect their belongings before you go."

"That's it then, Captain?" the Frenchman demanded.

"Yes, Captain, that is it," Grafton added in a short voice. "I think we have been more than fair with you under the circumstances. I could have sent you and your entire ship's company to the bottom."

"And my wounded?"

"Those that survive will be set ashore in the first French port we encounter or anywhere else they want to be let off." Grafton looked to Mr. Dobbs. "Get them in the boats and shove off," he commanded, still aggravated and short tempered, before he jumped across to the deck of the Tide.

He watched the French climb down the sides to the boats from the upper deck of the Bore Tide until all were aboard and pushed off. The lieutenant stood in his launch and saluted Grafton as they drifted away. Dobbs had given them several muskets, pistols and a keg of powder for protection on shore.

"How long a fuse did you set, Mr. Cole?" Grafton shouted across the decks of the ships.

"Twenty minutes, Sir."

"Light them, Mr. Cole, and get the men off." Cole sent the last three men back aboard the Tide and disappeared below to light the fuses. As soon as Cole came over they cut the ropes and the two ships drifted apart. Grafton shouted orders to the men aloft and the top sails unfurled.

Cole came up the steps to stand next to Grafton, Black and Elder, also on deck. "The men are exhausted, Captain. It's been a long day."

"Have the cook get the fires up and set a hot meal as soon as we dispatch that ship." Grafton ordered. "We do still have a cook?"

"Yes, sir," Cole smiled and went forward to set him to work.

They ran straight downwind away from the crippled frigate for fifteen minutes before Grafton brought the ship about and heaved to into the wind. He watched through his glass and the crew stood along the rail until a huge explosion ripped out the starboard side of the enemy ship and it listed hard over. Within thirty seconds the massive wooden lady completely rolled up and pitched over, nosing into the abyss under the roiling water.

"It's done, then," Grafton sadly commented to Black before he closed his glass. He looked back to the center deck. "Make way, Mr. VanDorn."

"Yes, Sir," he saluted.

"South by southwest if you please, Mr. Markell." Grafton said to the helmsman.

It was only eight in the evening when Grafton walked about his ship. Most of the men were quiet or already asleep. Doctor Morrison, with the help of Rita and Nelson Black, were busy seeing to the wounded which appeared to be an endless and daunting task. He found Mr. Martrovich with Major Bennett in his cabin drinking heavily happy they had survived the battle.

Grafton made his way up on deck to where Mr. Cole stood with the helmsman. There was a stiff breeze and the ship pounded against it on a tack course. "Mr. Cole, take the helm so Mr. Markell can get some sleep."

"I'm alright, Captain. No need for that, I'll stand my post," he objected.

"That's an order, Mr. Markell," Grafton pointed. "Go forward now and get some rest." Begrudgingly, the man let Cole take the wheel and went forward. Grafton leaned over the map table under the lantern's light and placed his finger on the shore line, without speaking its name, while Cole watched.

"You know that place?" He asked.

Cole knowingly nodded.

"Bring us about, Mr. Cole, so as not to alert anyone we are turning. Steer two points off north. The men should sleep through the night and hopefully this cloud cover will deceive them as to our course by day. Day after tomorrow we will approach the coast from the northwest so no one will know our real position is now miles north of the Baja tip."

Grafton stayed on deck with his first officer the entire night, calculating their course. Just before dawn he removed the compass glass and inserted two small magnets on the inside and watched while it swung around indicating a southern course. He looked up at Cole and smiled before he shut the instrument's case. Heavy, rain-filled clouds cooperated in the deception by covering the sky and the light remained grey and gloomy for the entire next day.

When Mr. Dobbs came for relief, he was advised not to question any abnormalities or say anything about the course he was told to stay on. The Captain and Cole finally were able to sleep most of the day, but relieved Dobbs and Markell before the sunset. Grafton refigured his course over and over throughout the night until he was satisfied they were in the position he wanted to be by dawn of the next day.

Thirty minutes before first light, they swung the ship to a southeast course into the sunrise and headed to the coast of northern Baja California. Grafton took the magnets out of the ship's compass before anyone came up on deck.

"We weren't more than kids the last time we came here with your father, Captain," Cole commented. "This was a very pleasant place as I remember, full of treasures."

"It's a smuggler's paradise, that's for sure," Grafton smiled. "It will be interesting to see if things are as we left them."

"You know Captain Beckett surely remembers this spot and if he hears about lost gold he could put two and two together to cause problems."

"We'll worry about that when the times comes. For now let's just lay over here for a few days, let the men relax on the beaches and make repairs. I doubt any of them can find their way back here to the gold even if they were to try." He leaned on the port rail to look to the morning sky. "If they come back with us, they can have a share in it."

Three o'clock in the afternoon brought a cry from the crows nest of land ho. Grafton glassed the coast and immediately realized he was exactly where he wanted to be. "Honduras, gentlemen," he lied and snapped the glass shut. "We'll put in to make repairs, unload some cargo and relax in the sun."

"You're really going to go through with it, aren't you?" Bennett snarled.

"Up till now I have not belabored the point, but by law, I am in charge of this operation, Major. Both on land and sea, as you well know, by a presidential command order. It is my determination, therefore, that for security of this mission all excess cargo will be secured on land so as not to fall into enemy hands."

Dobbs and Cole looked at each other in amazement at the remark, but said nothing. Elder rubbed his jaw while he considered this new information. "Guess we know now how you managed to get those Yankees off your ship out of Richmond," he said.

CHAPTER XI
COLORS OF A TRAITOR

Grafton maneuvered the ship into a small sheltered harbor and set anchor only some hundred yards from shore. It was a deep lagoon with cliffs surrounding three sides. For show he had one of the men sound the bottom but knew from experience the anchorage was no problem.

After a full day of rest for all of the men, Mr. Dobbs organized a shore party to re-supply fresh water and bury two of the wounded who had succumbed. Grafton and Cole took a launch and headed to one of the cliffs on the north side of the bay. They beached the craft on a narrow outcrop of sand next to the mouth of a cave, exposed only at low tide, and went in to explore.

"We had some good times playing in these caves, hey Captain?" Cole observed from the entrance.

"Indeed we did," he responded and walked further into the darkness. Wave swell rose and fell along a narrow rock path inside on the wall's edge, carving an opening about thirty feet in diameter and ten feet high. The pool of ocean water flooded in under the outer cave wall and was about five or six feet deep. The two men stood on the side and peered into the waters depths.

"Do you suppose it's still there?" Cole asked, "Your father's secret treasure chest?"

"Let's find out," Grafton replied and took off his gun belt, sword and dagger. He handed them to Cole. "You stay here," he said and dove into the water. It was crystal clear and the bottom was covered with rocks and dark coral. It only took a second or two for him to find the iron chain loop hidden in the rocks and pluck it up. He surfaced with one end and held it up. Cole set the weapons down and grabbed the loop from the Captain's hand. He pulled on it, bringing up another six or eight feet of links.

The chain was connected to a massive iron trap door three feet by four feet and covered in ocean bottom. The chamber underneath was four feet square and five feet deep. "It's open," Cole exclaimed.

Grafton dove back under and moments later he emerged with a sail cloth bag, handing it to Cole. He pulled himself out of the water and sat on the edge of the rock ledge. Cole knelt down and opened the laces before he poured out the contents into his palm. "Beautiful, aren't they," he smiled.

His hand was filled with several pearls both white and black and perfectly shaped. Grafton examined the booty, using his finger to sort about the items in Cole's palm before he looked up and smiled. "It's all there, just as we left it, the pearls, gold coin and silver bars." He held the bag open so Cole could return the treasure. "Tomorrow," he said. "We will add a couple million in gold bullion to it."

Nelson Black stood in the launch with his arms outstretched to catch the basket of food Rita had prepared. She slung it down before climbing over the side herself to join Nelson. Rita sat in the back and held onto a parasol for shade while he rowed the craft to the south shore. It was a glorious afternoon under a bright California sun and warm shore breeze.

They made shore and secured the boat, then searched the low dunes out of sight of the Bore Tide for a likely spot to picnic. Rita spread the colorful cloth on the sand next to a large rock outcropping in a shady spot and set out their feast. They spent the better part of an hour talking about nothing and enjoying the day. Nelson lay on his side supporting his head with his forearm and hand, where he could watch Rita's face while she sat next to him on her knees.

"Do you suppose there is anywhere else in the world as beautiful and pleasant as this place?" She looked at her surroundings and sighed, "In the entire world all I've ever known has been hostile and savage to black people and I have seen so many die for nothing but vanity." A tear formed on her cheek and Nelson wiped it away before he sat up next to her.

"Joe Elder speaks of a place beyond the frontier in America where few people live and no laws of civilization yet exist. He says it is life at its best with no one to control another man's actions and only the strong can survive." He pushed her long hair back from the side of her face. "We could go to that place and be free."

"I would go to the ends of the earth with you," she gently smiled, "You only have to ask."

Nelson bent down and kissed her on the mouth and she responded in kind. The innocent touch unleashed a passion that neither of them had the willingness or desire to stop. They each let their passions run free, locked together as one on the sandy shore, until they were completely spent and sated. Never had Rita felt so fulfilled and at peace with the world and as for Nelson, he now knew where his destiny lay.

Nelson's pants were rolled up to the knees as he pushed the boat out into the gentle surf with Rita aboard and hopped in. It took twenty minutes to row back to the ship and secure the launch. Rita straightened her clothes and fussed with her hair after she crossed the rail to the deck. Several crewmen stopped work to stare at the black female and when they made eye contact she coyly smiled with the knowledge they could only assume. When Nelson appeared they all went back to work.

The ship's repairs were well under way and the Captain called Major Bennett, Doctor Morrison, Mr. VanDorn and Flanders to the poop deck where Mr. Cole, Dobbs and Elder were already assembled. "Gentlemen," Grafton began, "We are going to transfer one hundred boxes of cargo into a cave which Mr. Cole and I found the other day over on that face of the north shore."

"Captain, that's a little over five million U.S. dollars," Bennett protested.

"I know how much it is Major, but it will be safe there for the time being and we can always retrieve it later. The men will load one launch and you, Major, with Mr. Elder, will row it over while Mr. Cole and I store it away. On the last trip I want you to bring Doctor Morrison and we will make an accounting of all boxes left, both there and on the ship."

"Such explicit record keeping could hang you, Captain," Bennett grumbled.

"None the less it will be done. Our crew now consists of twenty three men with some still in hospital. When we are finished, four boxes will be brought up on deck and broken open where each man will be given a bar of his own as bounty payment for their valiant efforts in taking the French ship." He looked at his crewmen who began to smile broadly, "You will see each man gets an equal share, Mr. VanDorn."

"Thank you, Captain, and the men thank you as well, Sir."

"No need for that," he nodded. "They've earned every ounce of it."

Grafton and Cole rowed over to the outcropping and waited for the first load to arrive. The four men set the boxes off on the sand and two returned for another load. The first twenty boxes were quickly opened and Cole handed bars to Grafton who placed them in the underwater chamber. They resealed the small crates after filling them with sand and stacked them against the back wall of the cave.

By the time the second shipment arrived, everything was secured including the heavy iron door over the loot. They continued to pile boxes on top of the empty ones, concealing the substitutions. It took most of the afternoon to get all 100 boxes piled into the cave and on the last trip Doctor Morrison was in the launch to confirm the count. Before leaving, they filled the cave entrance with rock and sand to conceal the opening when it could be seen.

The five men returned to the ship and counted a remaining two hundred and forty-six boxes. As promised, Grafton had four boxes taken up on deck where the men gathered and each man received his share. With the exception of the wounded, everyone was gathered on deck. "We will be here for two more days at most," Grafton informed them. "During that time, no one will be allowed to leave the ship to go ashore." He paused in thought, "I want this ship ready to sail, around the horn if need be, by the time we reach our next destination, Panama City."

"We will unload our cargo there," he continued, "and transfer it to Colon where the Breakwater is waiting to take it back to Washington." The men were silent but very attentive. "We lost many friends on this voyage and it has been a costly journey, but now it is winding down and those of us left will be able to enjoy a better future because of their sacrifice."

Grafton looked over his men. "Thank you all for your hard work and courageous actions against the French. Without it we could not have succeeded. When we arrive in New York I'll see you also get your sign on share of the fifty thousand I promised and then you will be free to go."

"Is it over, Captain?" someone shouted from the crowd.

Grafton looked over the men in silence before speaking again, but this time with a word of caution. "It's never over until you are ashore in your home port. Remember this men," he eyed them, "when you sit on ten million dollars of gold there will always be someone willing to die trying to take it away."

****

They sat at anchor for another day making repairs and Grafton grew impatient because November was quickly slipping away and he had two hundred miles to make up from the journey north. At last they were ready and Mr. Cole ordered the anchor hoisted early on the morning of the twenty-fifth. Much to Grafton's delight there was a stiff southerly breeze. The men aloft set sails and the craft silently slipped out of the harbor. Within minutes the ship was pounding into the swells and the sails were full. "South by west if you please, Mr. Cole," Grafton commanded. "Take us out of sight of land."

Nelson Black stood on the upper deck with his arms folded across his chest enjoying the morning air and the pitching deck. "Well, Nelson," Grafton asked. "What do you intend to do with your freedom and your share? I believe you have become a rather wealthy man."

"I have always been free, Alexander," he smiled. "And riches are in the heart not in the pocket." A far off look crossed his face. "I believe I will take Rita for my own and see what adventures might be found in the American West. It's a vast land, according to Mr. Elder, with free and savage people wandering everywhere. Strange, exotic animals and snow covered mountains higher than anywhere else in the world." He paused and nodded, "I would very much like to see it," he said, "before it is gone."

Grafton leaned over the rail and placed his hands together. "You would, huh." He looked out to sea. "There will always be a place for you with me on one of my ships if you change your mind." His eyes wandered over the horizon, "I have always wanted to ply my trade in the South Pacific around the Solomon and Gilbert Islands. Perhaps I will venture into those waters and enjoy the Polynesian atmosphere." Both men stood silent and thoughtful about far off dreams.

At last, Nelson reached out and touched Grafton's shoulder. "You fear this isn't over, Alexander, and there is more death yet to endure, don't you?"

Grafton stood without facing Nelson to answer, "Unfortunately, my friend, you are more insightful than you know." He looked into Black's eyes, "There may be many nightmares beyond the horizon which we must yet face and I don't even know what they might be."

Grafton and the able bodied men followed a daily routine of sailing the ship and seeing to the wounded. Several were nearly recovered and ready to return to duties while only four remained critical. Six of the Frenchmen were up and about as well and two, who spoke English, had requested to join the crew and not be returned to France. Grafton assumed it had more to do with a gold bar than any kind of ship loyalty, but he agreed only if they performed their duty for the rest of the voyage.

The closer the ship got to the equator, the warmer the weather and the better the crew's spirits became. It seemed to help aid the doctor in his administering to the wounded as well and it now appeared all in hospital would recover from their wounds.

On the 13th of December, 1863, the lookout shouted out, "land ho at two points to starboard," right where Grafton expected it. By the time they anchored just off shore, the sun fell behind the horizon and Grafton called his officers together.

"We'll lie over tonight, Mr. Cole, and see the cook gets out a hot meal for the men," he paused. "It may be their last for awhile. Before dark, get all the cannon and Gatling guns primed and loaded."

"You expecting trouble, Captain?" Bennett asked.

Grafton did not answer him but instead looked to Mr. Dobbs. "I want you and Mr. Elder to take a launch to shore and reconnoiter the town. Go have a couple of drinks in the taverns and listen to what the locals are talking about. I want to know if any strangers are about and what they've been up to." He pointed his finger into Dobb's face, "No trouble! Just get the information and be back here by twenty one hundred hours," he cautioned.

"Anyone sitting on ten million in gold had better expect trouble or they're liable to lose it," Grafton said, looking at Bennett. "Tomorrow we'll unload and cross the isthmus by train or wagon to the Breakwater, depending on what these two discover tonight."

"How will we divide the crew?" Cole asked.

"I'll take Elder, Black, Bennett and twelve of the crew with me and the rest will remain here on the Tide with you and Mr. Dobbs." He thought a moment then added, "I want Masters among those who come along as well. Everyone is to be heavily armed from now on, so break out the rifles and issue everyone a pistol." Grafton looked around, "Understood?"

"Yes, Captain," they all answered.

"Good, now see to your duties and set two men in the crows nest as lookouts."

It was a little past ten when Mr. Elder and Dobbs returned to the ship and the crew pulled the launch up the side. Both men went immediately to the Captain's quarters and knocked.

"Enter," Grafton shouted.

"Bad news, Captain," Dobbs blurted out no sooner than he was through the door. "Locals say there have been several unknown men about the streets in the past few weeks, Americans they think."

"Did you see any of them, Dobbs?" he asked. "They could be some of the Breakwater's crew."

"Maybe," Elder replied, "but we didn't see any of them for ourselves. One half-drunk Portuguese said they pulled out when we made port."

"Both of you get a good night's sleep for tomorrow," Grafton ordered. "And Mr. Dobbs, have two bell lines set down both rails to alert the sentries of any unwanted guests tonight. We'll start unloading before first light." He eyed his two men, "goodnight, gentlemen."

The sun had not yet broken over the eastern shore, but the sky quickly set a blue hue. Grafton had decided to take the gold by wagon where they could keep tighter controls than on the train. Elder found a man willing to rent eight draft animals for the day and he now sat on one of the readied wagons and waited for the Captain.

Grafton was about to board the launch when Bennett looked up from the boat and saw him stop to put his arm around Cole's shoulder. He wondered what information was being imparted to the first officer. His concern came from the fact that they had only unloaded half of the gold from the hold. The Major could smell a double cross in the air from his pirate conspirator.

Grafton stepped down into the launch and took a seat aft. "In command or not," Bennett said, "I will shoot you dead if you try to pull a fast one with the gold we have left on board, my pirate friend."

"Do pray you are a good shot, Major," Grafton smiled.

Everyone was assembled at the two wagons when Grafton climbed up next to Elder and they started off down the rutted trail for the town of Colon. It generally followed the railroad track along the fifty mile trip. They hoped to reach the Breakwater before darkness fell, which meant no stops except to rest and water the animals. Overall it was a very good road and the trip went well, that is, until they were just outside the town of Colon itself.

Grafton called a halt on top of a rise outside of town and glassed the bay where he could make out the Breakwater at anchor. "There she is," he said. "I can't make them out, but there appears to be a lot of activity both on the ship and at the docks." He wrinkled his brow and continued to look into the glass. "There is also a steamer at anchor beyond the reef and I don't like the look of it," he said before he shut the glass. "We'll go to that ledge on the side of this hill, he pointed, "down there by that stream and send a man ahead to have a look."

Elder slapped the horses with the reins and whistled without saying anything to start off down the hill. When they reached the small brook, they stopped in the cool air of the shaded ledge. Elder jumped down off the wagon and a seaman, Fitzgerald, moved up next to Grafton on the seat. All the birds and woodland creatures suddenly became silent and a deathly quiet fell over the scene and unsettled the men.

"I got a bad feeling, Captain," the crewman whispered and slowly racked the lever of his Henry rifle. Elder pulled his pistol and calmly turned to eye the jungle vegetation which hung close to the wagon next to him. The waterfall was more of a trickle cascading steeply away into a gorge on their left. Grafton looked to the right where a small meadow stretched about 30 yards before the dense trees started again.

A shot rang out and Grafton heard the musket ball pass inches from his cheek. It exploded in Fitzgerald's face raining blood and matter over Elder. More shots, then screams from the trees on both sides and Grafton could see his men drop from heavy gun fire. He immediately jumped from the seat, but as he did a pistol ball struck him in the back of his right calf and he hit the ground hard. Elder fan shot his pistol killing two men who had stepped out of the trees on their right.

Grafton struggled to his feet and could see Nelson behind the back wagon surrounded by Confederate troops. He pulled his pistol and looked between the horses and wagon where he could see at least a hundred uniformed men charging them from the meadow. He raised his side arm to fire but stopped when he suddenly recognized the Rebel Colonel directing men from the trees. He changed the pistol's angle to his new target and that's when he saw it.

The late afternoon air was humid and the sun glinted off the round musket ball as it left a vapor trail from the soldier's gun and came directly across the meadow at him. In slow motion Grafton watched the ball nearly hit the side of an advancing trooper then travel behind the horse's tail and the front of the wagon to strike him in the stomach two inches below the navel. He felt a sharp pain travel all the way through his body and shock his spine. The pain doubled him in half and pushed him backwards towards the high vegetation. All the while, he watched the Army Colonel shout out orders.

Grafton hit the ground on his back and rolled head over heels through the tall brush down the steep bank next to the creek. Everything remained a blur during the fall, which soaked him in the mud and wet foliage from the two hundred yard slide. He came to rest spread out on his stomach next to the river of the lower valley. A terrible pain continued in his mid section and lower leg. Just before everything went black, he thought the world seemed at peace and everything had somehow been set right.

Nelson Black had killed the eight men who first approached him from the near trees on the left, but now twenty or more charged from the right. He looked down the line and saw all were dead and Elder surrounded. He slashed to death the first two men who got close but realizing the situation was hopeless, he did a somersault into the brush and started a fast long slide down the muddy hill.

After he emptied his revolver, Elder pulled his knife and stabbed the next man out of the brush. Both men spun around while a second stepped up and shot him in the back. If he hadn't tripped the bullet would have killed him, but instead it passed through his shoulder. Joe turned and grabbed the rebel's arm before he could fire again and the two struggled over the weapon until he was able to thrust the knife into the soldier's side and both slipped over the edge and slid down the hill.

Masters was down on one knee, rapidly firing his lever action into the charging men, and Major Bennett stood over him. Suddenly, there was a loud thud which caused Masters to look up in time to see the

Major fall back and disappear into the brush with a bullet hole in his forehead. He quickly looked both directions and saw he was the only survivor and the Confederates let out a large collective holler as the firing subsided. He crawled to the edge and rolled down the slope before they detected his escape.

"Captain," he heard a voice. "Captain," the voice was there again. "Are you alive?" Grafton tried to focus his vision. "Captain, it's me, Joe Elder." The voice slowly became clear and so did his eyesight. The westerner bled profusely from his left shoulder. He was bent over holding his pistol with one hand and shaking Grafton's shoulder with the other. "We got to get the hell out of here before they figure out where we went."

Grafton half sat up to feel his painful mid-section by pushing his hand under his sash. He was surprised when he could see no blood on his shaking fingers. He took hold of his dagger and pulled it out sheath and all. The Confederate ball had struck the knife and bent it nearly in half in the case. He smiled at Elder, "Damn if it didn't save my life," he said and eyed the blood on Joe's shoulder. "You hurt?"

They heard splashes in the shallow river of someone running in the water and both men looked up stream. Elder turned his gun in that direction but lowered it when he saw the figures. It was Masters and Nelson Black, both unharmed. "It went clear through the shoulder," Elder said keeping his eye on the two men who got ever closer. "Over here," he quietly shouted.

Grafton got to his knees and found his pistol in the weeds. Masters was out of breath and dropped down on one knee when he got to the Captain. "They killed everybody, Captain, and took the wagons."

Grafton took hold of his shoulder. "You have got to get back to the Tide. Follow this river upstream until it's safe to go back to the road. Maybe you can even hitch the train, but get back to the ship as fast as you can. Tell Mr. Cole to follow his orders." He looked into the man's questioning eyes. "Mr. Cole will know what to do."

Masters looked at the blood pouring down the side of Grafton's boot but didn't say anything. Grafton lurched forward with a sudden pain in his gut but looked up. "Get going, Mr. Masters," he struggled to get out, "and stay with Mr. Cole."

"But Captain," he protested.

"Go now, before those Confederates get there ahead of you and try to take all the gold." Begrudgingly, Masters got up and started up river while the others watched until he was out of sight.

"It's good to see you well, my friend," Grafton smiled and grimaced at Nelson. "I am afraid Mr. Elder and I will require your help."

Nelson looked at his surroundings, "It would be best if we get out of here Alexander. Can you travel?" He asked and handed him a Henry rifle for a crutch.

Grafton took the rifle but looked at the weapon with a question on his face.

"It was Major Bennett's. He and I both fell down this cliff as you did, but I'm afraid he is dead along with all the others."

Grafton put the barrel into the mud and held on to the stock to help him stand. "We'll head north east up those hills," he pointed, "back to the seas of the Atlantic."

By night fall the trio was in a hidden saddle on the upper side of the mountain overlooking the town of Colon. Nelson took stock of the injuries to each man. Elder was weak from loss of blood and had begun to sweat profusely. Most of the bleeding from Grafton's leg had stopped, but he too was exhausted. Nelson set the two down by a small fire and went in search of water and food.

He returned in short order with water and two birds for cooking. They tore up Grafton's fine silk shirt to fashion a bandage for Elder. Nelson then took off Grafton's boot and cut the pant leg up the seam to examine his wound. He rolled the flesh in his fingers. "It's got to come out, Alexander."

Nelson broke off and cut up a small brush limb. He put it in Grafton's mouth and told him to turn over onto his stomach. "I am sorry, my friend, but this is going to hurt like the very devil." As soon as the sharp knife cut the skin of his leg, Grafton clenched down hard on the stick and used all his courage not to cry out. Seconds later, he passed out from the pain.

The small fire crackled and a gentle warm breeze flowed past the campsite. Grafton realized he lay on his back in the dark and two men sat across the fire from him. "Looks like he's back with us, Nelson," Elder smiled.

"Did you get it out?" Grafton said with a rough voice and

swallowed hard.

Nelson smiled and tossed a small pistol ball onto this chest. "You're lucky it wasn't a musket ball or I would have had to saw off that leg." He got up and brought Grafton a drink of water and a roasted fowl leg.

He took the drink and looked up at Nelson, "Any idea what our Confederate friends are up to down in town?"

"Hard to see in the dark but there was a lot of activity earlier." He handed him the food. "Eat."

"I might give you my leg to know what's going on down there," Grafton coughed and took the food.

Nelson stood up and removed his sword, sash and turban. "Take good care of my weapons Alexander, I'll be back by morning to claim them."

"Maybe you could pass as a poor black slave at that," he smiled and said before Nelson stepped into the dark. "As long as you keep your English mouth shut," he hollered after him.

"What difference does it make, Grafton, if you know what's going on down there or not," Elder grumbled. "It appears we'll be marooned here for the duration anyway."

"I never liked that word, Mr. Elder."

Both wounded men were asleep when Nelson quietly returned to the camp and he left them alone until the sun broke the horizon. He re-stoked the fire to heat water and clean their wounds because he was sure Grafton would have them on the move again. He knelt by the fire to soak and stir the silk cloth when he noticed that the Captain watched him in silence.

"That town is alive with Confederate troops, Alexander, and they plan to mass for a train trip this morning to take on the Bore Tide. It seems they are not happy about the amount of gold in our wagons." He stood up and dropped his stick. "Yesterday, when the train arrived in town, they waited in ambush, but of course we weren't on the train, were we. That's when they moved to the glen and waited for us to come up the road." He shrugged his shoulders. "They do believe they killed everyone with the wagons."

"If Mr. Masters made it back to the Pacific, the Tide has long since departed and will not return." Grafton sat up and dusted off his coat.

"In any case, we can't worry about them now because we have our own doings."

Elder looked up from his position on the ground, "Just what doings are those?" he asked.

"Getting that gold back for one," Grafton replied, "and we must take care of that Goddamn traitor for another."

"What traitor," Nelson asked somewhat confused. "Do you mean Beckett?"

Grafton did not answer, but instead struggled to his feet and painfully hobbled around the fire to stretch his sore and swollen leg. "We'll make for that higher ridge," he nodded in the general direction, "and have a look to the northeast up into the next bay."

Elder glumly looked up the steep wooded mountain slope and sighed. "That's a mighty tough climb, Captain. What do you expect to find up there?" he asked. "And while we're at it, just how do you propose the three of us get back that gold from several hundred Rebels.

"I expect to find salvation on that ridge, Mr. Elder, and the means to retrieve our property."

Nelson cleaned the wounds of both men and redressed them with the hot silk cloth before they began their journey to the summit of the higher ridge. The climb was arduous for all, but it was especially hard on Grafton with a leg wound. By four in the afternoon they sat on a fallen tree at the top, exhausted and nearly spent.

Elder turned from the downed trunk he sat on and looked out to the bright blue Atlantic Ocean sparkling in the afternoon sun. Grafton also turned seaward and looked out through his glass. "Is that a ship I see in that far bay?" Elder quickly sat higher and excitedly asked.

"Indeed it is," Grafton smiled while he surveyed the area.

"Can you make her out?"

He snapped the glass shut and looked at both men. "I don't need the telescope to tell you what ship that is!" He exclaimed. "It is there on my orders and Captain Pender is seldom late." Grafton smiled at the confused looks he was getting. "It's the clipper, Rip Tide, out of Boston. My ship, gentlemen," he boasted. "I told you last night that I don't like the word marooned, Mr. Elder." He studied the slope before them. "We should manage to get down there sometime tomorrow if we travel part way this afternoon."

They collected themselves for a few more moments, then started off with a renewed vigor down the back side toward the ocean and rescue.

****

"You three look like hell," Captain Pender said with a smile when he saw the men climb over the rail from the launch. "It appears you have already met the Southern contingent bivouacked in Colon. You're lucky we spotted your signal and our look outs didn't shoot you themselves." He stepped forward and extended his hand to Grafton, "Welcome aboard, Sir."

"Thank you, Captain," Grafton replied. "I can think of no place I'd rather be at the moment." He turned to his traveling companions and gestured with his hand, "this distinguished looking chap is Nelson Black and my western friend here is Joe Elder." They each shook hands in turn. "Gentlemen, this is Captain George Pender of my ship the Rip Tide."

The Captain stretched out his arm aft, "My cabin gentlemen for some wine and a hot meal." He turned to his first mate, "Have Mr. Trimble bring his medical kit and fresh bandages to my cabin."

"At once, Sir," he replied and scurried off forward.

They all enjoyed the hot meal and fine wine before the medic looked at the wounds and pronounced both Mr. Elder and Captain Grafton would recover. Grafton stretched out on a couch in Pender's cabin and slept soundly for several hours. Elder and Black went forward to clean up and also get some sleep.

Captain Pender returned to his cabin in the early evening and found Grafton at the table drinking port while he examined his beautiful and ruined dagger. "Shame about that," he pointed at the bent knife in Grafton's hand.

"Rather this than me," he said and tossed it aside on the table. "Tell me where we stand and exactly what is your situation?"

"As you saw on your arrival, we are well concealed here by the fish hook jetty surrounding this bay, although we are a little close to the bank for my liking. We are also exposed to anyone crossing that high ridge you came over, but so far that has not been a problem."

He tossed his hat on the table and poured himself a glass of port before he sat down. "I've got two men on the outer shore of that jetty and they have a commanding view to observe any ship movement north out of Colon. There is one man up on that ridge who I am surprised you didn't come across, and I sent three men to the town itself."

"How long have you been here, George?"

"Just over two weeks now. The Breakwater and another ship, the Mississippi Duchess, sailing with her, were already in port." He shook his head, "I knew the minute my men came back with the news you were right about treachery. That ship was full of troops waiting for your arrival. We had a man in Panama City for a few days hoping to warn you off, but the other American became too suspicious of him so he pulled out." He looked up at Grafton with a sad look, "I never figured Beckett for a Judas."

"This plan was conceived in Richmond from the start, not Washington, but I didn't figure that out until yesterday. Act two was going exactly as planned until we didn't show up in Colon on the train with the gold. Captain Beckett is obviously a Southern sympathizer and was a part of this from the very beginning." Grafton took a drink and sat back in his chair.

"You see, in act one, a General Applegate was supposed to capture us on the beaches at Baja, steal the Tide before the French arrived and use it to bring the gold back to Panama. They would simply use my plan and transfer it to the Breakwater then sail to whatever southern port they chose unabated. It was never their intent to haul that much gold across the plains of Mexico."

"But I thought you…"

Grafton held up his hand to stop Pender's question. "I would guess this ship that accompanied Beckett to Colon was an after thought in case Applegate failed. The worse that could happen was the loss of a French ship; either way the money would end up here in Panama. With overwhelming force, they would simply kill us and take it back." He turned the wine glass in his hand. "The beauty of their plan is that no Union blockade ship will molest the Breakwater. Even now it remains a foolproof plan and they are safe to bring the gold into any port by one of my ships."

"Sounds like they thought of everything," Pender lamented.

"Except they ignored the fact that the man they recommended

to set this plan in motion was a pirate and had decided to steal their money," Grafton smiled. "We brought less than half over the trail and hopefully Cole has already set sail with the remainder." He leaned forward, "They only got five million and no chance to get it all, so soon they have to sail north and that's when we'll take it back." He emphasized

"Captain, there is no way we can go up against such a force even at sea," Pender cautioned. "I've only got four cannons and two artillery pieces on board. I didn't expect to get into any sea battles down here, you know."

"They'll sail together for protection but that Confederate scow will have to stop somewhere and refuel because she'll be dragging along slowly to stay with the Breakwater." He got up and went to a map on the Captain's wall. "My guess is they'll lay over here." Grafton pointed and tapped his finger on the depicted island. "The Breakwater will have to go on from there alone so as to not be molested by the blockade."

Pender came up and looked over his shoulder to see the island of Jamaica, West Indies at Kingston.

"Being a schooner, the Rip Tide is faster, no?" Grafton looked back at Pender but didn't wait for an answer. "We'll arrive ahead of their little convoy and hide the ship. We can then jump the Breakwater after the Confederates pull out. and give them a taste of their own medicine."

CHAPTER XII
FORTUNES LOST

On the morning of the 18th crewman Earl reported sighting the Confederate paddle wheeler steaming north with the Breakwater following. Pender sent urgent word to call in his lookouts and prepared the ship for sea. He and Grafton studied area maps on the aft deck to plan their best course around the two ships and how to beat them to Kingston. "We should leave on the evening tide just after sunset," Pender advised. "That will put us nine hours behind, but even with a circular course we will make that up in four or five days of sailing."

"I agree," Grafton nodded. "I know this is a long shot, but it's all we've got. You are right about not confronting them at sea, of course. I want revenge for the loss of those good men and it sticks in my craw they made off with the money." He smiled at Pender, "I don't like to lose."

Pender nodded and stood up straight, "We'll have to see that you don't then."

There was still light in the sky when the Rip Tide rounded the jetty under full sail and made for deep water. Winds were favorable for the trip north. "The ship is yours to command, Captain Grafton," Pender said and stepped aside from the helm.

"That will not be necessary, Captain," Grafton replied and spoke loud enough for the deck crew to hear. "This is your ship and your crew. Just get me to Kingston to fulfill my destiny."

Getting to Kingston became much tougher than anyone would have thought. Two days out of the Jamaican port, the Rip Tide encountered the back side of a West Indies hurricane and the seas became absolutely frightening. There was no way to maintain course and they had to run downwind with reefed sails which pushed them westward away from Jamaica toward San Juan. It took two days to come about, a day to repair rigging and then a tack course into the wind. All and all they arrived five days late at Kingston clearly behind the Breakwater.

Kingston was a town in shambles from the storm and had little services to offer. The Harbor Master did report that the Breakwater lay over twelve hours to wait out the back side of the storm. He thought they would head to Nassau for repairs and supplies. He said there were no other ships with her, and her crew did not come ashore. By his best estimate they had departed some ten to twelve hours prior.

"We can still run her down, Captain Pender," Grafton said and punched his fist into his palm. "We must depart immediately to beat them to Nassau." he smiled, "This is a great turn of events. Beckett would not be surprised to see the Rip Tide at anchor there and he most certainly won't be expecting to see me."

Pender turned to his first officer, "Mr. Peal, get us under way if you please. Your best speed to the Cuban coast." The man began barking orders to the crew as the sails slid up the three main masts and the craft maneuvered out of the harbor.

"I would like to have fifteen or so volunteers to accompany me, Mr. Elder and Black to board the Breakwater in Nassau. The best fighting men you have." Grafton stood next to Pender and looked over the men on deck. "Beckett's first officer is a coward as well as a poor leader and surely some of the men on the crew are only following his orders. I hope they will rally to my side when we appear on deck and the struggle will be short."

"They are a good crew and hard workers who have always looked out for my interest, but my men may not be very motivated to fight a battle, Captain. I would say there doesn't appear to be much in it for them but a possible death." Pender tipped his head, "I will be coming along, of course."

"Agreed, Captain Pender, and I sympathize. Therefore, I will personally guarantee every man who follows me a five hundred dollars bonus." He smiled, "That should put some iron in their backs, hey?"

"Very generous of you, Captain. I would think they will all want to go." Pender turned, raised his arm to Mr. Peal and told him to assemble the men on deck, which he did directly. When all were accounted for, Pender told them Captain Grafton had something to say.

"Men, as you know, I am in pursuit of the Breakwater. Her captain double crossed me in a business deal and stole my ship. I want it and the cargo back. This, unfortunately, will not be accomplished without a fight. The Captain would not expect that to happen in Nassau or from the Rip Tide, so we will have an element of surprise."

"However," he continued, "a fight of this nature is bound to be deadly and I will need fifteen volunteers to help out with this task. A show of hands, if you please," he smiled. Of the thirty men on deck nine hands went up and one man in the back asked what kind of cargo was so important.

Grafton turned and whispered, "Your men have more scrap in them than you imagined, George." Grafton looked back at the men. "Gold is the cargo on board that ship, but it belongs to the Union."

"Not if we get it first!" someone shouted and everyone laughed.

"Just because I struck a deal for the gold with the Union doesn't mean you shouldn't be rewarded for any efforts in its recovery, so I assure every man who helps me will receive a bonus of five hundred Yankee dollars."

A hum of conversation crossed over the crowd of men and all thirty hands went up in agreement to fight, along with a cheer. Grafton smiled and nodded, "Fifteen thousand dollars it is then." He turned to Captain Pender, "We must plan to take Beckett unawares."

"Let's retreat to my cabin and discuss this operation in more detail Captain," Pender offered. "My second officer, Mr. James Newton, has some thoughts along that line." He turned to the first officer who stood behind them, "Mr. Peal, send him to my cabin," Pender ordered.

"At once Sir," he replied and started forward until Grafton's voice stopped him. "Tell Mr. Elder and Black to join us," he paused, "Yourself as well, Sir."

Newton was a proper gentleman, graduated from Harvard College and always dressed impeccably. He was young and some crewmen mused a man not yet ready to shave, but wise for his years and very thorough in all matters. He promptly arrived at the Captain's door as ordered.

"Mr. Newton, Captain Grafton and the rest of us would like to hear your thoughts on retrieving his gold from the Breakwater," Pender informed him and offered a seat at the table with a hand gesture. "Some wine?" he asked.

"Thank you no, Sir," he said and removed his cap, placing it gently and squarely on the table. Newton walked up to the wall map behind Grafton, who had to readjust his chair to see. Elder stood by the door to watch while he nursed his shoulder and the others sat attentively at the table.

He put his finger on New Providence Island and tapped on Nassau.

"This bay is the only protected anchorage within reach of town, eight miles to the northwest. Therefore I would assume that is where Captain Beckett will lay over for repairs. Unless things have changed in the past two years, as I remember, there isn't much there. We should allow the Breakwater to make berth and start repairs which would render her un-seaworthy, and even if she were so inclined, not able to run."

"Further, I would propose," he turned to look at Grafton. "For insurance purposes only, we arrive first and unload two artillery pieces with men and canisters able to fire from shore. The shrapnel would wreck havoc with her rigging and crew, and with the Rip Tide in the bay, we would have them in a cross fire." He tipped his head, "Hopefully, none of this would be necessary."

"You have an alternative plan then?" Grafton asked.

"Yes indeed. It is my understanding from earlier conversations that Captain Beckett believes you to be dead, Captain Grafton, and he should have no reason to view the Rip Tide or Captain Pender hostile. If we arrive from the east, we could heliograph him and ask as to your whereabouts on approach into the bay. We could relay that Portsmouth dispatch requested us to search you out and check on your welfare."

Grafton shifted in his chair, "Please continue, Mr. Newton."

"Well, Sir, he will undoubtedly report your death and Captain Pender would request a meeting aboard the Breakwater to discuss the topic. We should stand off far enough to use launches, or cannon if necessary, and time this so he would board with Mr. Peal and I after dark. When they go below for drinks, I will distract the lookouts, while you, Mr. Elder and Mr. Black organize a boarding party."

Grafton stood to look closely at the map of New Providence and consider the plan. Newton could see he was interested in the proposal.

"If most of the crew is below and we take the officers by surprise, it would be possible to secure the entire ship without firing a shot." He paused and looked down, "I served with Captain Beckett for nearly a year and some of those men are friends of mine."

"All of those men are employees of mine, Mr. Newton, and have served me, as well as Captain Beckett, in fine fashion. This American civil war has divided our loyalties which both sides have used against us with the lure of gold." Grafton looked to Captain Pender, "This boy has a fine plan and we shall attempt to carry it out."

He glanced back at the map. "Now, let's beat the Breakwater to New Providence."

****

On the 30th day of December, 1863, the Rip Tide sailed north to stand off shore from the lagoon outside of Nassau and await the arrival of the Breakwater. She had left behind Joe Elder and five men to crew two artillery pieces from the bank. If everything went south he had orders to sink the Breakwater in place. Their wait was short lived because at dawn, the Breakwater dropped anchor three hundred yards from Elder's hidden battery.

They sent a launch ashore with several men who set off to town. Elder waited until they passed, then hurried to signal the Tide from the top of a tall sand dune by the use of a mirror. She was drifting ten miles east of Nassau and the crows nest lookout easily spotted the flashes. By noon of that day, the deck watch on the Breakwater saw the ship's approach and notified the Captain.

"Can you make her out Captain," Mr. Hecker asked while he nervously looked over Beckett's shoulder on the aft deck along with two of the crew.

"Huh," he shrugged. "It would appear to be the Rip Tide, Mr. Hecker. I wonder what she would be doing so far south?" Beckett thought out loud with concern in his voice.

"This is bad luck. There is no way Pender could possibly know about our last passage or our cargo, could he?" Hecker asked and fidgeted with his beard.

"No," Beckett lowered his glass and looked back at him. "Grafton gave him orders to sail to England before we left."

"Captain," crewman Harrison pointed. "She is signaling with the light."

Beckett went back to his glass to watch the flashes. He spoke to the others while he decoded the message. "They say they have been searching for the Bore Tide's whereabouts and fear for her safety. All contact lost after Boston, can you help." He closed the glass. "Mr. Hecker, signal Rip Tide that Captain Grafton is dead with all hands and invite them to make anchor."

"Captain, we know Grafton is dead, but not his ship and men."

Hecker cautioned.

"Damn it, she will be man, when the Mississippi Duchess catches up with her in the Gulf of Mexico!" His timidity angered Beckett as he growled back at Hecker. "Now get that message sent." he shouted. With a lower voice and cruel smile he softly said to himself, "I'll lure him to dinner so we can capture him and take his ship as well."

Beckett went back to his observation of the Rip Tide. "This isn't bad luck, it's a fortuitous opportunity," he mumbled.

"What do fortuitous mean, Captain?" Harrison, who still stood behind him waiting for orders, asked.

Beckett slowly turned and smiled at the man's ignorance before he answered. "It means I am about to inherit all of Alexander Grafton's shipping interests."

The Rip Tide slowed to a crawl before dropping anchor a hundred yards abeam the Breakwater. Pender left the aft sail set and the ship swung around presenting a perfect broadside position for a cannon shot, if needed. She was perfectly situated for the cross fire scenario they'd planned.

By the look of the rigging on the Breakwater, Pender estimated she could be ready for sea in one or two days. Especially, with the rate the crew was making repairs. "Trouble, Captain?" Pender shouted across.

Beckett turned and looked aloft to his sails and spars before he answered. "Bad storm out of Port Royal I'm afraid, but we'll have her sea ready soon enough." He raised his arm from his sides, "Sorry to have to give you the news about Grafton."

"How did it happen?" he questioned.

"Bring your officers and come to dine this evening and we'll talk." Beckett shouted the invitation.

Pender nodded, "We'll see you at eight!" he informed him with a loud voice.

Captain Beckett was feeling very confident about the gathering in his staterooms with the officers from the Rip Tide. He was entertained by the fact that Pender had dressed in nearly the same attire Grafton usually wore. He had planned the festivities well and had even armed several of his men. At a predetermined time, they would barge in and he would take the Captain and his officers hostage, thereby forcing

Pender to concede his ship without a fight.

They had discussed his concocted lie about the loss of Captain Grafton and the Bore Tide over the troubled voyage to Panama. Now Beckett rose from his seat at the head of the table and picked up his wine glass. "A toast," he exclaimed while he tapped the glass with a table knife, "To the valiant Captain Grafton and the intrepid crew of the Bore Tide."

The others stood and raised glasses before drinking but suddenly a shot rang out on deck and there was some shouting. Beckett smiled and set his glass down.

"Don't you think you should see what that's about, Captain?" Pender asked when Beckett did not respond to the shouts. Beckett threw his napkin to the table and turned toward the door when it unexpectedly burst open. Someone pushed a crewman into the cabin and he stumbled to the table where Mr. Peal caught him. Grafton stepped in the room immediately behind him with his pistol in one hand and his sword in the other.

The imposing Nelson Black stepped in next, with Beckett's first officer in an arm brace, and held him on his tip toes with a dagger to his throat. It was now that Pender and Peal both lifted their coats and produced pistols. Captain Beckett's conceited look turned to that of shock when he realized Grafton was still alive and stood before him.

"Captain Pender, see to your men on deck and order everyone topside," Grafton commanded. "Mr. Black and I will take care of these two."

He and Peal left the cabin and pulled the sailor along with them. Grafton put his sword down and picked up a glass of wine, smelling it before he smiled, toasted Beckett and drank it down in one gulp.

"Nice of you to bring my ship and gold through that storm in one piece, John," Grafton said.

Beckett dropped into his chair without comment, complete with a defeated look on his face. "So," he said and looked up, "what happens now?"

"Why, John?" he paused, "Why, after all these years did you betray me? I have always treated you right. I even gave you command of this ship out of respect for your ability and loyalty to my father." Grafton shook his head, "Don't tell me it was for the money."

"Hardly," he scoffed. "Being captain of a ship you don't command is not being a captain at all." He looked around, "This has always been your ship and you send it to do your bidding. After your father died, I could never accept you as the boss."

"To me you will always be that snot-nosed kid stumbling around the decks while mighty men like me," he pointed his thumb at his chest, "and your father commanded the seas. The South offered me much more than gold or money for my greed. It was my chance to have it all and they graciously agreed to make certain you were out of my way. I could care less which side wins this American war."

"Great risk should pay off with great reward, don't you agree?" Grafton stated. "Or great punishment if you fail." He looked to Black. "That is for others to decide. We'll have to see what happens as it is still undetermined how this adventure will turn out."

Grafton motioned for Beckett to stand. He pulled a short length of rope from his pocket and bound his hands in front of him while Nelson tied Hecker's hands behind his back. They took both men up to the aft deck. The crew of the Rip Tide had completely surprised the crew of the Breakwater and they now stood around the outside rails with the captured crew gathered in the middle. Grafton pushed Beckett in the back and he stumbled forward toward the poop deck rail and the other officers. A shot rang out from the rigging and Captain Pender fell next to Grafton.

Grafton immediately dropped to one knee to survey the top sails where he spotted Jennings, the second mate, on the lower spar. He fired his pistol but the ball hit the mast sending splinters in every direction. His second shot caught Jennings in the collar bone but not before several other shots erupted from the deck knocking him from his perch. His bloody body fell the twenty feet to the deck into a crumpled heap.

He reached out and rolled Pender over. Grafton could see the spark of life was gone from his eyes. "Damn," he softly swore and looked up at a shocked Newton. "This was a good man and a long time friend." Grafton stood and had the look and sound of a man possessed when he addressed the crew. "Anybody else!" he angrily shouted. "You men there," he waved his hand to the left rail, "see to it no one else is armed."

One of the Rip Tide's crew bent over the downed Jennings and shouted up to Grafton. "He says it was you he wanted to shoot, Captain. Guess he couldn't see clear in the low light."

"Will he live, Mister?"

The crewman stood up, "No, sir, I'm afraid he's gone off, he has."

"Is there any man here who believes this is not my ship or that I am not its master by rule of law that governs the seas?" He slammed his fist into the rail not expecting an answer from the quiet group. "If you have any doubts, or the same idea as your prior Captain here about mutiny, I will shoot you where you stand." He stopped and took a second to calm himself and watched the men carefully.

One of them with a black eye and cut cheek, who stood in front, looked up at the Captain, "We were promised a trip bounty just like other times. These men were just following orders, Sir." He shrugged, "Nobody down here wanted to take your ship, Captain."

Then another beaten man joined in, "We been kind of scared ever since we heard those rebels killed you in Panama cause we didn't know what to do and," he stopped.

"And what?" Grafton demanded from the man. He also noticed that he, too, had been beaten severely, "And what happened to your face?"

"Well," he sheepishly answered, "Crewmen Meyers there has beaten any man in the crew who dared speak out, so the rest would stay in line. He was Captain Beckett's henchman, Sir."

Grafton looked to the man he'd indicated and it was easy to see why the men feared him. He was a huge man with muscular arms and a scarred, pockmarked face which gave him a mean look. He stood with his arms crossed and a defiant sneer came over his face when his eyes met Grafton's. "That man there?" He pointed and several men nodded their heads.

Grafton swiftly drew his pistol and fired one shot, striking the surprised man in the forehead. He dropped dead to the deck. Hecker began shaking uncontrollably in Nelson's grasp and wet himself just before he passed out.

He glanced over to the fallen man then back to the crew. "There will be no further beatings or mistreatment of any kind from the ranks.

I am the first, Goddamn it, and I'm the law!" he screamed. "You will agree to follow my orders or I will leave you on this island to rot."

He looked at the dead man and pointed to the first sailor who'd spoken up. "Get that shit off my deck and throw it overboard." Several others gladly joined in and they pitched the body into the water where it made a loud splash in the quiet air.

Grafton stood silent for a moment and his voice calmed, "I will see to it that you men receive the bounty promised and hold no grudge against any man who does his duty from this point forward, so speak now of your intentions," he paused. "What say you by show of hands?" The men looked around, then everyone raised an arm and shouted their loyalty. "So be it."

He leaned on the rail and looked at one of the marked men, "What's your name, sailor?"

"Jacob Morgan, Sir," he replied and thumbed his brow.

"I know you, do I not, Mr. Morgan? As I recall you are an educated man with a long history aboard this ship?"

"Yes, Sir, ever since Captain Beckett took command, Sir. Been at sea 25 years and I can read, Sir." He quickly answered.

"What cargo do you have in the hold?" Grafton inquired.

A broad smile came across Morgan's face and his eyes lit up for the first time. "Gold, Sir, and a lot of it."

"Very well," he smiled. "You are hereby appointed my first officer for this trip and I want you to pick a second. After the men get a good night's sleep, clean off this rigging and ready the Breakwater for sea.

"Yes, Sir," the stunned man replied. "May I ask, Sir, where are we going?"

"New York, Mr. Morgan." Grafton turned away and saw that Beckett was staring at him. Hecker had recovered and struggled to his feet.

"You going to shoot us, too, Alexander?" he raised one brow.

"No Sir," he paused, "I'm not." Grafton looked at Nelson, "Take them below and see to it they're placed in chains. When you're finished Nelson, please see if you can find Mr. Elder and have him come aboard."

"Mr. Peal, you will command the Rip Tide for now. Mr. Newton will be your first officer and I want you to follow us to New York."

Grafton started to walk away but stopped. "Oh, and leave five armed men aboard the Breakwater tonight for security just in case. We will set a wide course and swing out away from the coast and the blockade ships to approach from the east. Understood?"

He sadly looked down at Pender's body, "You may take your Captain back to his ship and prepare him for burial. If you'd like, I would be honored to read over him."

"I think the Captain would prefer to be buried at sea and not in this dingy harbor atoll. If you don't mind, Captain, we'll put him to rest after we make sail."

"As you wish," Grafton nodded and walked away.

CHAPTER XIII
NEW YORK WATERS

Mr. Elder came aboard but had left his men with the artillery pieces on shore. He made his way to the Captain's quarters where he found Grafton pitching some of Beckett's belongings out the aft portals.

"This man was a complete slob when it came to housekeeping," Grafton commented when he realized Elder stood in the doorway. "You'd think he would have at least seen to a decent steward."

It was clear to Elder that Grafton was agitated and genuinely upset. "I was extremely sorry to hear about the death of Captain Pender. I know he was a good friend of yours."

Grafton stopped what he was doing and looked at Elder, "Thank you, Joseph, for your concern and yes, he was quite dear to me." He dropped the items in his hands on a table before he continued. "George Pender hired on out of San Francisco to work as a crewman for my father. It was right after the voyage where we'd rescued Nelson and his Master, Langston. He wasn't much older than Cole and I, but knew a hell of a lot more about sailing than either of us."

Grafton turned his back and looked into the black window, remembering. "My father took us back to Europe where Bass, George and I finished our education. The year after Oxford we were trading goods and sailing the Rip Tide in the Mediterranean when my father fell ill. He named me Captain and bequeathed all his holdings before he died on board. We buried him off Gibraltar where he still lays and watches out over the seas. Beckett got nothing and that set him off, but he didn't do anything about it."

"We returned to Holland where I bought the Dutch Eagle and renamed her the Breakwater." He lifted his arms and looked around at the ship, indicating where they now stood. "I made Beckett her Captain, which in hind site seems to have been a mistake."

"I preferred the Bore Tide, which was the newest ship of our fleet, and it was uncommonly fast for its design. "I named Pender Captain of the Rip Tide which also stuck in Beckett's craw because that's the ship he wanted. In any case, we came to America because I felt trouble looming on these shores and there is always profit to be made in war."

"Your Civil War finally broke out and we started doing alright, at least until I got involved with taking sides and the pursuit of 14 carat gold. Too bad George won't be around to enjoy the riches." He turned to see Elder silently watching him.

"I did not mean to bore you, Mr. Elder." He changed the subject and cleared his throat. "I would like you to have some of the crew load the cannons in the morning. Mr. Morgan is the new first officer and he will see to your needs. As soon as that is done and the decks cleared, we will sail for New York."

Elder turned to open the door without comment but stopped and looked back. "I was not bored, Captain. You have made me a relatively rich man and I don't know whether to thank you or curse you, but I am sorry about the loss."

"You're a good man, Joe Elder, one of the bravest I've ever known, and I have been proud to have you at my side during this endeavor." The two men exchanged eye contact before Elder pulled the door open and left.

The late afternoon brought a good northwesterly wind and a high tide. The cannons had been loaded as Grafton requested and everything secured for sea. Not trusting the ability of his new first officer, he took the ship out of harbor himself and set a course away from the American shore.

The Rip Tide followed at a distance with only half sails so as to not overtake the slower ship. Grafton stood alone on the aft deck of the old craft. A wind brushed his hair and he could sense her days were numbered as a viable trading ship. It was a new era where steam and steel commanded. That would be the way of the future for anyone serious about plying a trade on the seas.

He also watched the waters to the south and wondered about his first officer and the Bore Tide. All he could do from this deck was to fret and worry about their fate, and he had to decide what to do about his treasonous Captain Beckett. Surely, he thought, there must be others on board who had sympathy for the Southern cause.

Mr. Morgan stepped up next to Grafton and looked aloft. "She's got her wind now, Captain, and she'll serve you well." He cleared his throat and glanced back at him, "no need to worry about the men anymore either, Sir. After that unfortunate situation with Mr. Jennings and Meyer," he paused. "Now the men are afraid of you, as well as Mr. Black and Mr. Elder.

"That was not my intent, Mr. Morgan, but I did act rashly the other night. Please pass the word they have nothing to fear from their officers. I want good men who work for honest wages, not fearful slaves." He took a long breath still lost in thought. "Have Mr. Beckett and Hecker brought up from below decks to get some air and a decent meal." As an after thought before he left, Grafton added, "Tell Mr. Elder to keep an eye on them," he ordered.

The 19th of January brought light winds with drizzling rain along with poor visibility. Captain Grafton stood on the command deck at the front rail where he could observe the crew as they made ready one of the long boats. He signaled for Mr. Morgan to come up the steps from the main deck. "Is the Rip Tide still in sight?" He asked."

Morgan turned to look aft, "It is, Sir, barely."

"Have the crew assemble on deck if you please, Mr. Morgan, and close reef. We are going to heave to."

Somewhat confused, he nonetheless followed his orders and within five minutes the ship's progress had stopped and everyone was assembled in front of Grafton. "Mr. Black," Grafton requested, "would you be so kind as to bring Captain Beckett and his first officer to the deck."

Everyone looked around at each other with a sickening thought that something very bad was about to happen to those men. When the two reached the deck, Grafton ordered them to be untied. He looked back at Elder and asked him to bring up the box which sat on his cabin table.

"These men risked everything to destroy me and lost," Grafton started. "As Captain, I have found them guilty on all counts and the time has come for their punishment." He looked over a sullen and quiet crowd, while Mr. Elder came up from behind with the small chest. Grafton took it and tossed it over the rail to Beckett.

"As of right now, Sir, we are eighty one miles due east of the Chesapeake Bay," he said. "There is a sail and provisions in that long boat. That chest contains maps, compass and sextant. I intend to set the two of you adrift and you may go where you will with nothing, except your lives."

Beckett looked at the case and back up at Grafton, stunned and did not know what to say.

"If I take you to New York, the Yankees would surely hang you as traitors or, at the very least, throw you both in the Pea Island jail forever." he shrugged, "At least this way you've got a chance, slim as it may be."

"I did not expect this from you, Alexander," Beckett finally managed to get out. "I thought you a brutal man with no mercy."

"I won't be the one to kill you John," he replied, "I don't want your blood on my hands. Besides, your years of service to my father must stand for something. Who knows, perhaps, you'll get a medal or they'll find you a Confederate scow to command."

Grafton looked up and over the crew. "Any man here is free to go with them." He leaned forward with his hands on the rail. "If you so choose you may take your share of ship's bounty promised and wages, as I hold no grudge against anyone and would wish you well."

The men looked around at each other and a murmur raced over them about the offer at hand. After a few moments, four men raised their hands and one of them spoke up, "You said we can take our bounty, Captain?"

"That's right," he answered.

The man nodded, "Alright then, I want to go, Captain. My home is up on the James River and I'd like to see the old folks before they die."

Grafton stood up and turned, "See to their shares, Mr. Morgan, and get some men to help put that launch in the water." He looked back at his men, "As soon as they are away, make sail," he ordered.

After the launch was out of sight, Grafton changed course and signaled Rip Tide they were bound for Wilmington, Delaware. With the slow hull design of the Breakwater and tacking the entire course to landfall, it took seven days to make anchorage abeam Fort Dupont in Delaware City. They tied off to a wooden pier and he ordered the Rip Tide to lash on to their side. The position wasn't to the liking of the Harbor Master but he, nonetheless, allowed them to remain in that configuration.

Grafton left Joe Elder and Nelson Black in command of both vessels at dock, which surprised even Peal. No one or any cargo, he ordered, was to leave the ships. He made his way to the fort gate to seek an audience with its commander. The sentry took him to the Colonel's adjutant, a Major Raemus.

"Major, this here gentleman would like to speak with the commandant," the sergeant explained, in the stone built office of the inner post wall. The major stood and extended his hand.

"I am Major Raemus, the adjutant and officer of the day, Sir. How may I be of service?" he asked

Grafton spoke as he reached into the upper part of his left boot. "I am Captain Grafton of the Bore Tide and recently returned from a mission for some people in Washington City. He pulled out his commission paper and handed to the Major. "Perhaps, you recognize the names on that document?"

Grafton was silent while the Major read and looked up in utter disbelief. "I've never seen anything like this before Captain, I mean, Colonel." He lowered the letter in thought. "May I take this to my Commander while you wait?"

Grafton nodded and tipped his hand, "Of course."

He waited in the outer office with the Sergeant for only a short time before the Major returned with his Colonel. The man extended his hand while the Major stood at attention.

"Colonel James Austin at your service, Sir," he smiled. "What is it we can do for you?" he asked and handed the commission paper back to Grafton.

"Captain Grafton, Sir, of the Bore Tide," he replied as they shook hands. "I docked two hours ago outside of Delaware City with two ships, the Breakwater and Rip Tide. I own these vessels as well and of late have been under the secret commission of Undersecretary of War Mr. Nathan Stepp. I must now journey to Washington and report."

"How does that concern us, Mr. Grafton?" The Colonel looked somewhat confused.

"I need a detachment from your fort to place my ships under Martial Law and quarantine them until I return. I want no man, cargo or contact of any kind between land and my ships while I am away."

"Well I am not sure we can exactly…" he began before Grafton cut him off.

"I do not wish to belabor the point, Colonel, but my powers in this matter are absolute and come directly from the President. I would greatly appreciate your assistance without having to make demands," he raised one eyebrow.

"How many men would you require, Sir?"

"Ten armed men and one officer should do the trick. They are also authorized to shoot any man who tries to leave."

"And just how long will you be gone, Captain?" the Colonel asked.

"I would hope to be back by tomorrow night or morning of the next day at the latest and relieve your men."

"Very well," he nodded. "Major, see to this immediately," he ordered, "and return with the Captain to ensure everything is to his liking before he departs."

"You have been most gracious, Colonel, and I will be sure the Secretary hears of your outstanding cooperation," Grafton smiled and saluted him.

Grafton returned to the ships with the detachment of soldiers and spread them down the dock. The Harbor Master was again not pleased but elected not to interfere with the Army's presence on his pier.

"Men," Grafton addressed the gathering of crew on deck, "I have duties which will take me to Washington for a couple of days. In the mean time you are all confined to these ships under Martial Law until I return." A grumble went up on both ships. He looked around, "It is an unpleasant fact of life, to be sure, but I must insist. To stress how important it is that you remain here, I have ordered these Army guards to shoot any man who tries to leave." That remark completely silenced the group.

Grafton had ordered a carriage which arrived on the dock as he spoke. "Mr. Peal, you are in command of both ships while I am away and I expect you to keep these men busy. There is much to do. I want the Rip Tide ready for sea when I return."

"Yes Sir," he shouted from the deck

"Mr. Elder," Grafton asked. "Do you have our equipment?"

"Indeed I do, Captain."

"Very well," he gestured for him to leave the ship and looked up. "Mr. Black, if you please." The three men made their way to the coach where Grafton thanked the Major for his cooperation then looked to the driver, "Your best time please to Washington D.C."

"Yes, Sir," he replied, "We'll be there by midnight."

Members of the displeased crew watched the coach disappear and eyed the soldiers left on the docks. A light rain began to fall and most of the men returned to the cabins.

****

Joe Elder, along with Nelson Black, came to Grafton's rooms at seven AM in the Washington Hotel. He was already dressed and had eaten breakfast. "Grab the valise there on the desk will you," he said to Nelson and drew his pistol from its holster. He checked the chambers for load and spun the cylinder. He smiled and put the gun away, "Now let's go see Mr. Stepp, shall we."

Secretary Stepp sat at his desk, having a pleasant cup of morning tea with his teenage daughter. Two men shuffled papers on a back table and grumbled about all the undone tasks. Suddenly the door burst open and a startled Colonel stepped through. "Mr. Secretary, you must come out here at once and see to this!" His voice shook with urgency.

Stepp rose from his chair when he heard the Captain's voice, "No need for that, Colonel," Grafton said and barged past with Mr. Elder and Black in tow. "Good morning Nathan," he smiled. Stepp's facial expression revealed shock which amused Grafton.

He looked back, "These are my associates, Mr. Elder and Mr. Nelson Black."

Secretary Stepp cleared his throat when he looked at Nelson, "You look exactly as Captain Grafton depicted you," he said in amazement.

Nelson tipped his head but did not answer.

"Forgive me for being surprised, Captain, but the latest information I had; you were killed in Panama, your ship with the gold was in New Orleans and your associates had betrayed you."

"Hardly," Grafton said and spied the beautiful young lady who sat next to the Secretary. She smiled when their eyes met and he noticed they sparkled like jewels in the night.

"Why, father," she giggled, knowing he was uncomfortable with her speaking at all. "He looks just like the pirate you described."

"I am a pirate, Lass," Grafton snapped his heels and bowed.

"I suppose good manners dictate I should introduce you," Stepp acknowledged. He turned his open palm to the girl, "This lovely young lady is my daughter, Elizabeth."

"Charmed," Grafton exclaimed and tipped his head again.

"Since you're not dead, Mr. Grafton, I quickly deduce that neither is your ship in New Orleans. So where is the gold?"

Grafton did not answer but instead turned to the valise Nelson held out. He reached in and tossed an ingot bar on the desk which hit with a crash, marring the top, as slid all the way across. "My word," Stepp exclaimed, as he looked at the sparkling bar.

"There are several thousand more of those on my ship at dock in Delaware City, under guard of the U.S. Army." Grafton smiled, "thankfully they know not what's aboard. I suggest you send an appropriate force to recover it."

Stepp looked to one of the men in the back. "See to that at once," he sternly ordered the underling. "Did you get it all?" he asked.

"The bulk of the gold is on the Bore Tide under the command of my first officer who had to flee the Panama Isthmus after we were attacked. It may be some time before he arrives in New York, if at all."

"Damn!" Stepp exclaimed while he shook his fist and smiled. "I could not be more pleased about this turn of events." His jovial attitude subsided when he remembered his daughter. "Oh, I am sorry, my dear," he apologized.

A side door opened and Lieutenant Overton stepped into the room with his head down, reading a paper he held. He looked up, smiling, but when he saw who was present the grin disappeared and an ashen pallor came over his face. Before anyone could react, Grafton pulled his pistol and fired one round. It struck Overton in the right leg just above the knee. He dropped to the floor, screaming in pain, and Elizabeth let out a short gasp.

"My God, Sir, what is the meaning of this?" Stepp yelled. Several Marines rushed into the room, hearing the shot, but stopped when Stepp held up his hand.

"Mr. Black, if you please," Grafton indicated with the barrel of his pistol that he wanted Overton in a chair. Nelson pulled him up and dropped him into the seat then stood next to him with a massive hand on his shoulder. Overton held his wounded leg and rocked back and forth in pain.

"Someone fetch my surgeon," Stepp ordered.

"If this man utters one lie he will not need a doctor, Sir, but an undertaker." Grafton growled. Stepp did not notice it, but his daughter was all but dazzled by the dashing and formidable man before her.

"I demand to know what this is about," Stepp shouted.

"He is the traitor among you. I didn't figure it out myself until Panama." Grafton turned to Overton. "What is your name, Lieutenant?" he calmly asked but got no answer. Elder smartly drew his pistol and fired a shot, grazing the man's cheek.

"Joshua James R.C. Landry, Colonel of the Mississippi Lancers and you should be dead. I saw you fall myself," he exclaimed and all the while rubbed his leg.

"All of this, Mr. Secretary," Grafton explained, "was his idea from the beginning. He set it all up by feeding you the information and suggested using my ships because one of my Captains belonged to him. I saw him last in Panama where he directed Confederate troops as they attacked our convoy. Providence prevailed and I was not able to kill him there." He looked at the trapped man, now crumpled in the chair. "When did you get back, Landry?"

"Just three days ago," Stepp interjected. "It was he who reported on the progress of your mission, or should I say its failure and the loss of the gold. He's been on one of his intelligence gathering trips, or so I thought."

"I'm sure he believed the Breakwater went to New Orleans and it almost did but I intercepted it and took it back. Even as we speak his ships are searching for the Bore Tide to capture or sink her with the remainder of the gold. You see I double crossed Captain Beckett and didn't deliver it all as they expected. In Baja, after I observed the Confederate forces sent to collect their money, I realized we had a traitor in our midst." He paused, "All along, I thought it was Bennett or you," he looked at Stepp, "until Panama."

"I take it Major Bennett is still with the Bore Tide and the gold?"

"Major Bennett was killed in Panama along with twelve members of my crew by this man's regiment," Grafton informed him. He raised his weapon, pointing it at Landry, and slowly cocked it. "There is no

Confederate ball to stop me now Overton." The wounded man closed his eyes and he grimaced waiting for death.

Stepp quickly looked up to the Marine guards, "Get this man out of my sight and hold him for treason before the Captain shoots him."

"What about his wounds?" One of the men asked.

"Get him out!" Stepp screamed and pointed to the door. They shuffled around and removed the Colonel from Stepp's office. "The rest of you clear out, too." He said to the room full of onlookers from the outer office while Grafton slowly holstered the gun. "Please wait outside with Mr. Douglas, my dear," he softly said to his daughter.

Elizabeth's eyes stayed on Grafton when she walked past. After everyone had filed out, Stepp looked at the three men. "I owe you gentlemen a debt of gratitude for the success of this mission."

"No," Grafton said, "You owe me one hundred thousand dollars upon the safe return of the Bore Tide."

Stepp smiled, "Indeed, what do you propose we do next?"

"Nothing, I intend to wait," he wrinkled his brow. "It is the only thing we can do. Bass Cole is a good man and remarkable sailor. If the trip can be made he can do it. I ordered him to go to New York if anything went wrong in Panama, and it did thanks to Landry and my Captain Beckett."

"What about this Beckett?" Stepp asked. "Do you have him in irons?"

"I set him free. He probably headed to Richmond along with some of his crew."

"I want him hanged," Stepp insisted. "Why in the world would you let him go?"

"A debt of honor, and besides, he is not an American, Nathan." Grafton glanced at Elder. "While we are on the subject, some of my men have gold in their possession and I don't want them harassed about it."

"It wasn't your place to give out that gold, Sir," Stepp protested.

"They earned it, some of them with their lives and you wouldn't have any of it if it weren't for their valor against incredible odds." Grafton leaned forward and placed his hands on the Secretary's desk. "With the Bore Tide's return and your payment, our agreement will be complete. There is slightly over ten million even after the bounty payment to my crew. It was my decision and my prerogative to reward those men and I'll hear no more about it."

Grafton straightened up with his hand on the butt of his pistol and his fingers twitched against the ivory handle. "I strongly suggest you don't try to double cross me in this matter, Nathan."

Ignoring the threat, Secretary Stepp dropped into his seat, "Ten million in gold," he smiled. "That's excellent, just excellent," he said and shook his head. "At last we're winning on the battle fields and now their economy will remain in shambles. The President will expect a full written report of your exploits, Captain. He may even request an audience." Stepp looked to the three men, "We should celebrate this occasion."

"I'll share that sentiment when the Bore Tide is at port in New York." Grafton turned to leave, "Good day to you, Sir."

CHAPTER XIV
A MISS STEPP

Grafton had settled into a flat with Mr. Elder, one street off the wharf, where he could easily monitor the comings and goings of shipping in New York harbor. After an extensive search of the more exclusive shops of the city, he managed to have his dagger repaired back to its original beauty. He also replaced his tattered clothing and had a custom overcoat reconstructed from the original.

The Breakwater had been dry docked for repairs and the crew transferred to the Rip Tide at anchor in that port. Several of the men left his employ at Delaware City to seek other ships or spend their gains. Mr. Peal was in command for the moment, though most of the men were on shore leave. Mr. Black found accommodations on the ship preferable to anything he could secure on land, so he remained aboard as well.

Grafton promised him a speedy return when the Bore Tide arrived with the person he most sought, Rita Perez. However, days turned into weeks and there was no sign or word of the Bore Tide. Even Grafton began to worry when the 12th of May passed and the days wore on. He knew the ship should have been back by the middle to the end of April, at the latest. Perhaps, he thought, they'd run into the doldrums off South America again and lost precious time or worse, came afoul of a Confederate ship.

On the following Sunday morning a messenger arrived at Grafton's door with a note from Nathan Stepp. It was a request to join him and his daughter at the Waldorf Hotel for lunch. He cleaned up, caught a carriage and arrived at the dining room shortly before one. The *matre'de* took him to the appropriate table in back.

"Ah, Captain," Stepp rose. "So glad you could join us," he gestured for him to take a seat and sat himself. "You remember my daughter, Elizabeth?"

"Of course," he nodded. "Always a pleasure to see such a beautiful lass in a fine dress," he complimented.

She blushed momentarily and stood up. "If you will excuse me, Sir," she said and looked to her father, "Father." Both men rose before she left the table and Stepp watched Grafton's eyes follow his daughter out of the room. When he turned back it was obvious Stepp was not amused and even somewhat concerned.

"Regretfully," he started, "I must admit, my daughter is quite taken by you, Captain." The men sat down. "I'm here on business. She insisted on coming along to shop and had hopes she might see you again. You'll find she is a headstrong girl and since the loss of her mother," he paused and raised an eyebrow, "Well, raising her has been a difficult task."

Grafton said nothing while the older man squirmed in his chair from his uncomfortable situation.

"I must respectfully ask your indulgence in this matter, Captain, and for your word as a gentleman not to take advantage of the situation. Though she doesn't look it, Elizabeth is merely fifteen years old and not yet savvy to the ways of the world. She doesn't believe that of course, but she is still a child and is an innocent."

He cleared his throat, "Secretary Stepp, it is my intention to leave these waters as soon as practicable for the South Seas. I've had enough of your country and I've been embroiled in its war far too long." Grafton folded his hands on the table. "One must experience it personally, but there is a kind of serenity and peace to be found in paradise and around the islands of Tahiti and Samoa."

He looked away with sadness in his eyes. "Sailing is about to fade into history. The tall ships and mighty men are all but gone. However, there is still a need in the islands for such men, so it is there I will sail." He looked back into Stepp's eyes.

"Your daughter is a beauty and on the verge of becoming a woman. Any man, including me, would be proud to have her at his side. She is intriguing to say the least, but I shall not steal her away and you can be assured her virtue is safe."

Stepp took a breath of relief and nodded. "Thank you for that, Captain," he said as Elizabeth returned to the table and both men stood up. "Shall we dine?" he asked and watched while Grafton seated his daughter.

Their meal was first rate and the conversation enlightening for Grafton as to the intelligence and charm of Miss Stepp. She was advanced beyond her years and well studied about current affairs. She also was interested in and eager to experience the customs and rituals of Europe. He had to remind himself that this was just a lass of fifteen.

Secretary Stepp and Grafton were about to finish a glass of port when the *matre de* announced that a messenger was out front for the Captain. He excused himself and left to see to it. A few moments later he returned to the table

"Secretary, Miss Stepp," he bowed. "It has been my pleasure but I must beg your pardon; it appears my ship has been sighted in the outer harbor and duty calls."

"Oh, father, may we go to the pier and watch? I've never seen a pirate ship," she mused for the Captain's benefit.

"Well I..." he started before she interrupted.

"Please Captain," she pleaded. "I, we promise not to be a bother."

Grafton raised and eyebrow and gestured toward the door. "Yes you will," he smirked, "after you Miss."

The Secretary stood up and dropped his napkin on the table. "Very well Elizabeth, we shall go see your pirate ship." He shot a stern glance at Grafton. "Perhaps, the pirate ship will have some pirate gold aboard."

Grafton found Joe Elder on the wharf watching the harbor with his glass and ordered the carriage driver to stop. The three stepped out, which caused Elder to turn. "She's about to cross over the stern of that steamer and dock in this berth."

He handed the glass to Grafton and eyed the pretty girl holding his arm. Grafton could clearly see the top sail of his ship and felt a great relief. Cole stood on the aft deck giving commands to attach to the harbor launches for tow before he looked up and waved to his Captain.

They finally tied off and put out a gang way so Grafton could board. He double stepped up the board to the rail. "Permission to come aboard, Mr. VanDorn?" he asked the man at the top of the rail.

"Permission granted, Captain," he smiled. "It's good to see you well, Sir," he beamed.

Many of the men gathered around to shake hands. Hobson, Quinten and Haskel, were all there, and welcomed him aboard. "Come now, men," Grafton quipped, "Mr. Cole certainly wasn't that poor of a

Captain." Everyone laughed as Cole made his way through the crowd and extended his hand.

Their eyes met with a brotherly knowledge of each other's feelings and shook hands. "Glad to have you back Mr. Cole."

"Glad to be back, Captain, and it is good to see you in one piece."

Mr. Stepp, his daughter and Elder came up the plank behind them and Grafton turned to make introductions. Cole suggested they retire to the Captain's quarters for a drink and conversation.

Grafton stepped into his cabin and looked around, "home," he said softly and smiled.

"I didn't use it, Captain," Cole informed him, "It is just as you left it."

"And the gold," he asked, "Is it where I left it?"

Cole knowingly smirked, "Yes, Sir," he nodded, "exactly where you left it."

"Outstanding," Secretary Stepp muttered over their shoulders.

"Mr. Dobbs," Grafton smiled, seeing his older second officer appear at the door. "I am so glad to see you survived this ordeal."

"Thank you, Captain," he bowed his head.

"Would you inform the men they are not to leave the ship until Secretary Stepp has his soldiers secure their bounty from the hold." He paused, "and would you also ask Miss Perez to join us."

Dobbs looked to Cole with a nervous twitch in his eye.

"I am afraid Miss Perez is unable to join us; she is extremely ill with fever and is being tended by Doctor Morrison."

"Will she live?" Grafton gruffly asked.

"The doctor is not sure," Cole informed him, "She was injured in Panama as we left port. Her wound fails to heal and she struggles, on and off, with some sort of infection. Of late she has again fallen ill."

"Mr. Dobbs," Grafton said, "I know it has been a long voyage for the men but as soon as the gold is unloaded we will put to sea."

"Where are we going, Captain?"

"Delaware City where the Rip Tide and Breakwater are docked. We will find Mr. Black," Grafton ordered. "Mr. Secretary, if you would be so kind as to immediately inform the Army Commander to remove your property from my ship, I would be obliged."

"Come, Elizabeth," he ordered, "I am afraid our plans must change and we will return to Washington immediately."

Grafton placed his hands behind his back. "You and you daughter are welcome to sail with us to Delaware. I know it is somewhat slower than the train but she can tell her grandchildren she rode on a pirate ship." Grafton smiled.

"Please do, Father," she begged.

"Alright," he agreed. "It would afford the Captain and I an opportunity to discuss business matters." Stepp rose to leave, "I will return shortly with a detail of men." He looked directly at Grafton, "Do take good care of my daughter while I'm gone, Captain."

Grafton clicked his heels and slightly bowed before Stepp left. "Have a seat, gentlemen," he gestured toward the mess table and eyed Stepp's back, wondering what he had in mind, "and tell me about your journey Mr. Cole."

"We were attacked by a small party of men shortly after you left. It really wasn't much of a fight because they didn't know about the guns." Cole raised an eyebrow, "Unlucky for them but fortunate for us as we only lost two men and Ms. Perez was shot in the abdomen." Masters returned to the ship that night and told us about your encounter and the loss of our men. I departed immediately and followed your orders."

"What took you so long to get back here then?" Grafton asked.

"Many things," he shrugged. "First was the Horn. We struggled for nearly two months and almost lost the ship trying to make the passage." Cole leaned back in his chair. "Mr. Martrovich died there, some say from fright, but the doctor said it was age and excess drink."

"Masters said you'd found the Breakwater and another ship in Colon. The more I considered that fact, the more I felt sure they would try and get us somewhere in the Caribbean or maybe when we approached the coast. After the Horn, I decided to go to the Azores for supplies, get rid of the Frogs, and then follow the trade winds." He gestured with his hands, "We swung around and approached more from the northeast. We never saw another ship either and avoided the blockade altogether."

"I am curious, Captain," Cole asked. "What happened to you out there and how in the world did you manage to retrieve the Breakwater?"

"Before we left New York some months back, I met with George and arranged for him to meet me north of Colon in Panama, but remain undercover. You see, I feared treason was on the brew and it came in the form of Bennett's aide. Anyway, we chased the Breakwater north and caught up with it in Nassau where I took it back."

"Sorry to hear about Bennett," Cole interjected.

"Worse yet, Bass, George is dead. Mistakenly shot on the deck of the Breakwater when its second officer tried to kill me."

"What!" he exclaimed.

"I shot him dead for his trouble. We buried the Captain at sea a few days later and came here to wait for you."

"Lord, hard to believe George Pender is gone," he shook his head with a tear in his eye. "We had some times together and that's for sure."

A knock at the cabin door brought Mr. Stepp back into the room, with a look of relief when he saw his daughter sat quietly between the men. "Your Mr. Dobbs is about to assist my troops in unloading the cargo. He was also rather vague about some other government property you have and its whereabouts. I would like to have it back, Captain," Stepp insisted.

Grafton looked to Cole, "Mr. Cole?" he asked with a raised eyebrow.

"Thirty five repeating rifles were lost in fighting both in Baja and Panama. The others are crated below. I believe all the ammunition was spent between practice and combat."

"And my Gatling guns, Sir. Where are my Gatling guns?"

"Two washed overboard in the waters off the Horn," Cole smiled, "It was a terrible scene to behold."

Secretary Stepp was not convinced but he was hardly in any position to press the matter. The unloading continued for the next two hours while other crewmen again readied the ship for sea. In the mean time, Grafton and Elder returned to their room on shore and collected their belongings.

The tide was on the rise at eight o'clock when they cut the ship free and set sail down the channel for open water. Grafton had visited with Rita and Doctor Morrison before they left port and tried to convince her not to give up. She drifted in and out of consciousness and he found her partly delusional. Three days or less, he promised, and she would be reunited with Nelson.

Grafton gave his cabin up to the Secretary and his daughter for the short voyage and bunked in with Mr. Cole. After the ship was set on course and the Stepps secure in their cabin, Grafton called the crew to the forward mess. Joe Elder stopped the last man in the door and told him to post it.

Grafton sat at one of the front tables. "Mr. Cole informs me, and I see by this formation, that we are few in number. Fourteen men by my count," he said. "I'm sorry about your friends I lost on Panama. It is only by Providence that the four of us survived." He drew a sad breath. "However, our numbers are sufficient to manage this ship and return to Baja."

One of the men spoke up. "Masters said you were wounded pretty badly. We thought you might even be dead."

"So was Mr. Elder, and if it hadn't been for Nelson Black, we would have died. He played a great part in saving both of us."

Mr. VanDorn spoke up next. "None of us much fancy going back around the Horn again, Sir."

"As you may recall," Grafton started, "we left some boxes on the beach off the west coast of Mexico." The men looked at each other and a murmur went around the room. "That gold belongs to you men and I think we should retrieve it. You risked everything, and most of your friends paid everything, so you have earned every bar."

"What about the government man on board? Doesn't he want it back?" Someone asked.

"He got the number of gold bars he expected and is happy about the sum. Of course," Grafton laughed. "If I were you I wouldn't mention the surplus when he's around." The crew also let out a nervous laugh.

"We gonna steal that gold for ourselves?" VanDorn asked.

"The simple answer to that question, Mr. VanDorn," he paused and looked at each man, "is yes."

"When do we sail?" came the response from the crew.

"We'll put things to order in Delaware and re-supply the ship for immediate departure." Grafton stood up from the table. "There is one more thing gentlemen. We, all of us here," he looked around, "are going to take a blood oath as brothers in this quest. No one will utter a word about our mission or destination. Is that agreed?" Grafton made each man individually swear an oath to a code of silence before the meeting broke up.

Grafton lay down on the small bunk in Cole's room and blew out the lamp. In the dark, he told Cole to keep Stepp busy in the morning until he had a chance to talk with the doctor about their quest for the gold.

Cole agreed, then spoke up, "The extra guns and ammunition are secured in the bilge. I figured two Gattlings and some repeaters could come in handy for the future," he informed him.

"I knew they weren't lost and so does Mr. Stepp," Grafton sighed before he fell asleep.

Morning brought a hearty breakfast in the Captain's mess for all officers and guests. The steward busied himself clearing the dishes as the social meal broke up. "Captain, if I might have a word in private?" Mr. Stepp asked.

Grafton eyed Cole at the door. "If you would be so kind as to see to that other business we spoke of, Mr. Cole?" he asked.

Cole merely smiled, nodded and walked out.

"What may I do for you this fine morning, Mr. Secretary?"

Stepp waited until the last person was out of the room. "The other day I mentioned my daughter was taken with you and I believe it may be a mutual affair."

"What are you suggesting, Sir?" Grafton sounded annoyed.

He held up his hands, "No offense here, Sir. I have only the best interest of my daughter at heart and her welfare after I am gone." He stopped and looked into his half filled coffee cup. "It takes a lot of money to educate and raise children these days and I know you are a wealthy man." He sat up, shifted in his chair and cleared his throat. "I also believe you are about to become much richer."

Grafton smirked, "You mean the money your government will pay out?"

"No," he looked up. "I mean with the gold you will retrieve in California."

Now it was Grafton who was uneasy, "I don't know what you're talking about," he lied.

"Come now, Captain. We're both intelligent men and only two

people in our government knew the exact amount of gold in that shipment," he paused, "myself, and Lieutenant Overton." Silence filled the room and neither man spoke. Finally, Stepp shook his finger in Grafton's direction, "You are a very intuitive man when it comes to spotting ulterior motives, such as greed. There was no point in my revealing the exact amount earlier as it seemed prudent and in my interest to let things simply play out."

He smiled, "You returned the stated amount and, after Overton is hung as a spy, no one will ever be the wiser as long as I am silent."

"For the sake of argument," Grafton speculated, "let's say there was some residual product left behind. Exactly what is it you want for this so called silence?"

"What else," he smiled. "My daughter's security is paramount to me, and I want your assurance she will be looked after, both morally and financially, should anything happen."

"The price?" he insisted.

"Quite simple, actually, I would want an equal share."

"I could kill you now and take it all," Grafton quietly laid out the threat.

Stepp swallowed hard, "If you did that my daughter would never forgive you." He slowly spun the cup on the table. "Also, I thought you might have a reaction such as that so there are certain provisions in my will, should I meet an untimely end." He smiled and looked at the Captain. "Is it so much to ask?"

"Agreed then," Grafton stated flatly, "but only when I return, which is perhaps in three or four years."

Stepp thought a moment then rose from his chair. "You are indeed a pirate and scoundrel, Sir, but I would take your word over that of many other more trusted men with whom I deal." He held out his hand and they shook. "Done," he said.

"I hope you realize, Nathan," Grafton's eyes flashed. "You just took a blood oath."

****

By evening of the second day, the Bore Tide had made her way well past North Cape May on her way to Delaware City. Captain Grafton was alone on the aft deck with the helmsman, Markell, and watched the flashes from the cape light house. Elizabeth strolled up next to him to enjoy the spring air.

"Being at sea must be a wonderful way of life," she commented. "It is so peaceful and the world seems somehow fresh as when it was first created."

"At times," Grafton smiled.

"My father says you are going away and will not be back." She looked up with tears in her eyes. "Tell me that isn't true."

He turned to lean against the rail on his left forearm and studied her lovely face in the low light. "It is true. Very shortly I will be gone."

"Would you consider taking me with you back to Europe?"

"Elizabeth," he reached out with his palm and lifted her face to his and rubbed the back of his hand across her wet cheek. "You know I won't do that, lass. It would destroy your father and you're not yet ready for such adventures."

"Oh, but I am," she pleaded.

Grafton shook his head. "Have patience, girl, your time will come. Besides, I'm not going to Europe. We are going to sail the South Seas for three years or more."

She looked down at the deck for a moment then back into his eyes. She slowly leaned toward him until their lips met and they kissed. Her face was so close, their breath mingled. "When your adventure is through would you come take me away," she whispered. "By then I'll be a woman grown and you can take me in your arms."

He stood straighter and looked out to sea drawing in a deep breath. "I tell you what Elizabeth. If I am still alive four years from now, on the rising full moon, if you look out from the harbor in Boston you will see the sails of the Bore Tide." He smiled and looked back at her. "Of course by then, you will have found others your own age to care about and will want nothing to do with a salty old sea dog."

"You're wrong," she insisted, "I will think about our meeting everyday until your return."

"Elizabeth," her father called out when he reached the top of the stairs. "Oh, there you are," he said, spying the two on deck.

She stepped back from the Captain. "Yes Father," she said but continued to watch his face. "I was just getting some air and visiting with Captain Grafton."

He walked up to the pair and took his daughter's arm. "It's time we retired, my dear, because we'll have a big day in the morning. I must get back to Washington and secure the Captain's reward," he said and eyed the Captain suspiciously.

Grafton bowed his head at that remark and to Elizabeth when they walked away. She turned and looked back at the Captain. "I won't forget, I promise, I'll be there."

CHAPTER XV
A NEW COURSE

It was half past four in the morning when they dropped anchor a hundred yards south of the Rip Tide outside of Delaware City. "Mr. VanDorn," Grafton ordered. "Would you take two men across and fetch Nelson. Bring him here at once."

"Aye, Sir," he said and hurried forward.

Within a half hour Nelson Black climbed the side rigging and stepped onto deck where Grafton met him. "Bad news, Nelson," he informed him, "Rita is suffering from a wound in Panama and she is in a bad way." Their eyes met and a desperate look came over his face. "I'm sorry my friend," he said with forlorn, "she is with Doctor Morrison."

"Excuse me Alexander," Nelson said placing a hand on his shoulder to push past and head below.

The room was dark with only a lantern that flickered on a corner table. Rita was asleep on an open bunk and sweated profusely. The Doctor was softly snoring, passed out in an overstuffed chair. Nelson picked up the lamp to hold it high over Rita and examine her state while he bent over her. His massive hand gently touched her face and wiped away the moisture.

"Nelson," she hoarsely whispered without opening her eyes." Is that you?"

"It is I, my love. You are safe now here with me and it is time for you to get well. We have much to do."

She struggled to open her eyes and gaze upon his face. "It is you," she smiled then wrenched in pain from the cramps that plagued her. Nelson softly placed his hand on her stomach and the pain stopped.

The Doctor snorted in his sleep, which woke him and he quickly sat up. "Nelson," he cleared his throat. "Is she awake?" he asked and stood to see for himself. "For the life of me I can't understand why this wound won't heal." He pulled back the wrap on her stomach to reveal a bullet wound in her right side. "The shot went clear through but tore the skin and tissue here," he pointed. "She recovers then relapses and each time it gets worse. This time I believe it to be fatal."

"How have you treated this?"

"Laudanum mostly," he answered, "for the pain, and herbal teas."

Nelson quickly pulled open the door and shouted for Mr. VanDorn. Shortly the man appeared and looked down on the stricken Miss. He stood and grabbed VanDorn by both shoulders. "I want you to find Mr. Dobbs. Tell him to go ashore and find me some tree moss, damp tree moss." VanDorn looked somewhat confused about the request. "Do you understand me?" Nelson insisted and shook the man.

"Yes Sir, tree moss, wet tree moss," he stuttered.

"Now go, and hurry," Nelson insisted. He looked back at the doctor then bent down toward Rita. "No more laudanum, she must suffer the pain without the drug and we will need lots of very hot water."

Grafton and Dobbs knocked on the Doctor's door in less than an hour with a cloth bag full of moss. Nelson had soaked the wound by using hot wet cloth and cleaned it the best he could. The men watched while he dampened the moss with boiling water and, much to the Doctor's amazement, he pushed it into and around the wound. He wrapped her abdomen in a cotton cloth and tied the whole thing off tight.

"Why did you put that dirty fungi in her wound?" the Doctor inquired, with some contempt.

"I've seen it used before by the Japanese for sword and knife wounds. In some people cuts won't heal well, they think it is from dirt, like that on your hands, Doctor. The moss has some sort of healing power, I expect, but we must be careful to take it out and change it every few hours."

Morrison examined both sides of his hands and dirty fingernails. "Huh," he scoffed, "tree moss indeed."

"Doctor," Grafton said, "may I see you privately in my cabin while Nelson looks after your patient?"

"Certainly," he answered, still staring at Black. The two men made their way to Cole's quarters where Grafton turned up the lamps.

"Would you care for a drink, Doctor?" he asked, with the decanter half tipped to a glass.

"Please," he gestured.

"I asked you here to examine what you might do with your portion of the gold bullion we left in California." He raised an eyebrow as he finished pouring the second glass, "or if you had even considered the matter?"

Morrison picked up his glass and took a sip. "I have, and I believe we are talking theft here, are we not? Why would you think I would become engaged in that activity?"

"Greed and ambition, Doctor, are not entirely unhealthy attributes of man and we are all capable of experiencing it, no?" Grafton twirled the contents of his glass. "In case you were wondering, my government contract has been fulfilled and the agreed upon money should arrive any day." He tipped his head and toasted the man before he drank. "Lest you tell the authorities differently, I have assurances from highly placed officials there will be no further inquiries. So there is no theft, only bounty which rightfully belongs to us."

Grafton could see the wheels of thought turn over in the Doctor's mind. "As a matter of fact," he said and set his glass down. "I am mounting an expedition to recover our property and you, Sir, are invited to come along." He let the silence work in his favor for a moment before adding, "California is in need of quality physicians with means to build good hospitals."

"What about the other men?" he asked.

"Equal shares for everyone and they have already given an oath of silence. After we pick up the money, most of them will go to San Francisco. As for myself, I am headed to the South Seas."

The Doctor gulped down the last of his drink. "I will resign my commission tomorrow and sail with you for California, Sir." A broad smile crossed his face. "I always wanted to be a rich man. Thank you, Captain."

Five days after they anchored, a courier from Mr. Stepp came from Washington with a box of federal script and a note which Grafton took as payment. Mr. Dobbs had divided half the money up among the crew as promised and most of them were off the ship to spend some of their loot. By agreement they all decided to leave any gold on board.

That evening Grafton summoned all of his officers to the Bore Tide for a meeting. Since the men were gone they sat together in the forward crew mess. "Gentlemen," he began. "I have decided to shut down Grafton Traders Ltd and close out my trade routes." He looked around at the stunned officers. "However, the assets remain, namely the three ships along with the Portsmouth office and warehouses. But I am sure the compelling question is what is to become of all of you?"

"Any thoughts on the subject?" he asked.

Mr. Peal spoke up first. "Mr. Newton and I had hoped to sail together on the Rip Tide as before, trading between England and America."

"Out of the question," Grafton responded. "However, the Breakwater is well suited for rough seas and cold weather which abound in the North Atlantic. There is need of trade routes between Belfast, London and the rest of Europe. Do you agree?"

Peal nodded without speaking.

"I will make you Captain and Newton first officer of the Breakwater. You may keep seventy percent of the net profit as pay and in three years we will sell the ship for whatever the market will bear and split the money. Or perhaps, the two of you may prefer to buy out my third. The distances are shorter and you will be able to make more trips, generating greater revenue and competing with the steamers, at least for a while."

"We would need operating capital to start, Sir, and neither of us can afford that at this point," Newton interjected.

"What is in the safe aboard the Breakwater?"

Peal shook his head and tipped his palms up. "Since the crew was paid off and with the cost of repairs that are left, I doubt there will be more than two or three thousand dollars," he answered.

"I will seed your operation with fifteen thousand dollars of my own money, but I do expect a return, gentlemen." Grafton stood and held out his hand. "Do we have an accord, Captain Peal?"

"Well, shake his hand, man," Newton smiled and slapped his new captain on the back.

"Mr. Cole," Grafton turned from the congratulations. "I believe you have spoken in the past of starting your own company in the Pacific with passenger service between California and Australia."

"Maybe, now that I am a richer man that will be possible, Sir." He responded.

"I'd say so, Captain Cole," he smiled. "Being a clipper ship, the Rip Tide would suit that task well." He paused, "The ship is yours, Bass." He reached out and shook his friend's hand, "Treat her well and make my father proud of his tall ship."

"I," he stammered, "I don't know what to say, Alexander."

Without an answer he looked over Cole's shoulder to Mr. Dobbs who sat quietly at the end of a long bench. "Mr. Dobbs," he startled the older man who jumped in his seat.

"Which would you prefer to be, the first officer of the Rip Tide under Captain Cole or me on the Bore Tide?"

He stood up and looked away to avoid Grafton's eyes. "No disrespect, Sir, and please don't take offense but Mr. Cole and I have been together a long time."

Grafton nodded his head, "Commendable Mr. Dobbs. I respect loyalty and wish you only the best under your new Captain."

"Thank you, Sir." He nodded and sat down.

"It's settled then," Grafton stated and looked about the room at the men. "With your permission, Captain," he said to Cole, "I will sail with you as far as California at your earliest convenience. It is always comforting to have two ships during a dangerous crossing."

The men sealed their agreement with several toasts and a party which went on well into the night.

They returned to their respective ships the next day and began repairs. Mr. Cole and Peal began to recruit men in town to supplement ships' personnel for the Breakwater and Rip Tide. By the middle of June, all three ships were seaworthy and manned. The Bore Tide only had her original crew aboard. Though slightly undermanned, their mission was too confidential to take on anyone new.

The best news of all was that Rita Perez had recovered enough to be up and about. Most of the men, who already feared Mr. Black, now looked upon him in awe and some wondered if the devil was in him. It seemed he had the power to bring people back from the dead.

Grafton worked on the charts in his cabin when Nelson and Rita knocked on his open door. "Ah, my two favorite people," he looked up with a smile and gestured for them to enter. "What can I do for you this fine day?"

"We are leaving, Alexander, both of us," Nelson said. "We'll follow our dream of seeing an untouched land where people are not enslaved."

"You may be gravely disappointed, my friend, but I wish you all the luck in the world. I truly hope you two find the peace and happiness you deserve." Grafton held out his hand and they shook.

Black pulled his Samurai sword sheath and all from his red sash and held it out in front of his body. "A favor I ask of you, my brother," he said and shook the beautiful weapon. "Take this blade with honor and keep it safe. Protect it from dishonor and use it only for justice." His coal black eyes burned into Grafton. "Someday, I will return and take it back."

Grafton was awe struck and didn't know what to say. "I…"

"You are the only person I trust to keep the faith between us and honor this blade. It will be the symbol that our friendship can never be cut. You have saved me from a fate worse than death in Richmond and I shall not forget you."

"You know there is a share for you and Rita in California." Grafton swallowed hard and gently took the sword from Nelson's hands.

"You may take care of that for me as well."

"You know where my father's home is in Holland and my office in Britain. I shall leave you some money in the Bank of San Francisco if you are ever in need." Grafton looked up from the sword with a tear in his eye. "I shall miss you, my friend."

Black took hold of both his shoulders at arms' distance. "Think of me on occasion, Alexander." He said before he turned and walked out of the cabin and out of Grafton's life. Rita stood silent and said nothing but looked at the Captain and smiled before she followed Nelson out.

Grafton dropped heavily into his chair and set the Samurai on the table. He stared at the weapon and lowered his head, cupping his palm over his brow.

"Do you have a moment, Captain?" the voice of Mr. Elder startled him.

Grafton cleared his throat and Elder stepped into the room. "Left that with you did he?" Elder pointed. "Guess I should have never told him all those stories about the west, but he never stopped bothering me about it."

"And you, Mr. Elder, what are your plans?"

"I suppose it is time to get back to my horses. This damn war can't last forever and now that I have some money maybe it will be easier."

"Don't want your share in California?"

"I can't imagine me with that kind of money. I'm free and wander where I want." He smiled, "too much of anything is not good for a free spirit."

"That's too bad, Joe, as I had considered asking you to be my first officer." Grafton leaned back. "Interested?"

"What do I know about sailing?"

"I watched you learn about everything on this ship and how it worked on our last voyage. I can teach you navigation and the rest. You are a natural born leader and the men respect you. What more could I ask of a first officer?"

"I am not sure I could trade in my cowboy hat so easily."

"Well think about this. I am heading for the South Seas for the next few years. There is a land there known as New Zealand where a good cattleman could build up a vast ranch especially if he had seed money." He sat forward with his arms folded. "I saw it for myself, Joe, with my father some years ago, and it reminded me very much of your American west."

Before Joe could answer, Grafton stood up and smiled. "I don't believe a man such as you could turn down such a grand adventure. Welcome aboard, Mr. Elder," and they shook hands.

****

Grafton stood on the aft deck of the Bore Tide as it followed the Rip Tide in the early morning darkness. He watched the lights of Delaware City slip away and listened to the sounds of the men working behind him. Their noises barely registered in his mind; that was on Elizabeth Stepp and whether he would ever see her again.

For her part, she had arrived too late to see her Captain again and stood on the pier with her father. Tears gently rolled down her cheeks. "Father, I fear he will never come back to me and will be lost forever."

"Come now, my dear, I have every confidence the Captain will return," he squinted his eyes and rubbed her shoulders.

"How can you be so sure, Father?" she asked.

"He and I have the same visions when it comes to greatness and make no mistake, my darling daughter. He is both pirate and thief. "Oh yes," he smiled, "now that you are the prize, he will be back."